The Bronc Stomper

—⁓—

Douglas Rawling

ISBN: 1499184999
ISBN 13: 9781499184990

I

The sun was sinking to the timbered ridges of the Little Belts, so that Nathan Daniels had to shade his eyes to make out the features of the big man on the iron gray gelding. Both horse and rider were leaned down and trail worn, and both were powdered in dust. They had something else in common too, and young Daniels figured he could sum it up in two words; patient and tough. The man tried to speak, but his voice cracked from lack of use. He cleared his throat and tried again.

"You lookin' for a bronc stomper?"

Daniel's head lifted in surprise, as the speaker didn't fit the mold. Most bronc busters were smaller wiry men and a bit on the younger side. He didn't voice his thoughts though and simply answered, "That's right."

"I'm lookin' for work."

Daniels almost asked if bronc busting was his regular line of work, but something in the man's demeanor seemed to preclude questioning, so instead he motioned with his head toward the barn fifty yards to the south and said, "Go ahead and put your horse up, then come on over to the cook shack and talk to Barry; he's the foreman. The boys are just takin' supper so I'll tell Lee to set another place. I reckon you could eat."

The tall rider nodded his thanks, and without a word turned for the barn. Daniels watched his back for a moment, and then headed for the cook shack. The sun had now lost itself behind the mountains, and two long fingers of light reached eastward then disappeared as the air took on a welcome coolness. Stepping up onto the veranda, Daniels hesitated a moment before reaching for the door. He was a well-framed but slender young man who would need another year or two to put meat on his shoulders, and he paused, his hands on his hips and waited. Above the muffled hum of conversation he could hear the unmistakeable sound of Cliff Barry's raspy voice, and it grated on him. Barry would be predictably angry, and then Daniels decided he didn't care. He was the one hand on the place that Barry was powerless to get rid of. The conversation subsided as he entered, and he was reminded that, though he was part of the crew, he wasn't one of them. He took a seat at the end of the table, his face taking on an expression of practiced indifference as Barry rose to stand beside him. Cliff Barry was a solid neckless man whose hard eyes were the most notable feature on an ugly face.

"You're late," he said, not trying to hide the condescending judgment in his tone.

"Am I?"

"About two days' worth."

Chan Lee's teenage son stepped through the kitchen door with the coffee pot and Daniels remembered. Ignoring the man at his side he called, "Lee-two."

The timid boy turned quickly to regard him, submissive uncertainty in his eyes. Chan Lee's son had a first name no one could pronounce, and rather than try to learn it, the crew jokingly referred to the Chinese cook and his boy as Lee-one and Lee-two. Daniels had never heard the boy speak a word of English, but he seemed to understand it alright.

"Tell your pa to bring out another plate. We got company."

Lee-two nodded, set down the coffee pot and fled to the kitchen. Daniels turned back to Barry who eyed him questioningly.

"A fella just rode in who wants to be Howard's replacement."

"If he's one of them shiftless saloon trash you like to waste time with, I ain't interested." Barry's expression changed ever so slightly and he asked, "How is Howard?"

"Doc figures he'll make it so long as pneumonia don't set in. He's busted up pretty good though."

Barry nodded and was silent a moment. Then he said, "I was hopin' you wasn't late 'cause he'd took a turn for the worst."

Daniels shook his head. "The fella I mentioned must have followed me in from town. He got in about half an hour after I did, and the first time I met him was when he rode through the front gate."

The door to the cook shack swung open and the big rider's frame filled the doorway, a dark silhouette against the fading red of the sunset, and then he stepped into the lamp light. The door clicked shut and conversation dwindled to silence as, with eyes shaded by his hat brim, he surveyed the room. When his gaze settled on Daniels, Daniels motioned with his head toward Barry, who then crossed the floor to stand before him. Both men regarded each other in a silent standoff, and Daniels watched with interest. Then Barry spoke.

"Who told you we were lookin' for a bronc buster?"

"Nobody."

Barry, appeared taken aback by the man's answer, and he asked, "Well then how'd you know to come here?"

"Just figured you might be needin' one." When Barry's wrinkled brow betrayed an unspoken question, the big stranger spoke again. "I was workin' for the fella you bought that jag of ponies from over at Miles City."

Barry nodded, but clearly was still not satisfied. "You're not workin' for him anymore?" he asked.

It was an unnecessary question unless hinting at further explanation, but the big man simply answered, "No."

After a moment of silence Barry remembered protocol and motioned to the table saying, "Have a seat. We'll talk about it after you've eaten."

The rest of the crew were just finishing their meals as the tall rider took an empty seat beside Daniels. He nodded a greeting as he sat down, and Daniels responded in kind, then he settled into patient silence.

Lee-two came in and began clearing dishes while subdued conversation slowly took the room. Smokes were rolled and coffee cups topped up, and when Lee-two set a plate of stew in front of the quiet stranger, he turned and smiled his thanks. When their eyes met, Lee-two's went quickly to the floor, and he hurried off to the kitchen. The man tested his coffee, then set it aside and began slowly and methodically eating his dinner.

Nathan Daniels pushed away his plate, leaned back against the log wall, and had his first good look at the man's face. It was a strong face with a square jaw, dark with the beard stubble that matched the shock of black hair hanging over his forehead from beneath a Stetson that had once been black too. Somehow the face managed to convey a certain hardness and a quiet peace at the same time. It made young Daniels unexplainably ill at ease, but he stayed where he was while the rest of the crew filtered off to the bunk house.

Barry came over and took a seat opposite the big rider, turned and laid a meaningful look on Daniels, who ignored it and stayed where he was. A tired look of disgust washed across the foreman's eyes, and then he turned back to regard the stranger.

"You know why we're lookin' for a bronc stomper?" he asked.

The big man set his fork aside, swallowed, and after a brief pause said quietly, "You got a lot of horses that need to get broke, and with the round-up comin' you'll be shorthanded."

"How do you figure that?" Barry asked.

"I reckon this drought's got you short on grass and your cattle will be scattered far an' wide so as you'll have a time roundin' them up in time to make your drive. You won't be able to spare the man power. You'll be needin' fresh horses too."

Cliff Barry studied the stranger a moment, appreciating his perceptiveness. Then he asked, "What makes you think we'll be makin' a drive?"

The man slowly reached for his coffee, took a drink, put his cup back down and said, "I seen a lot of country on my way out here. Most of the grass in the basin is chewed to the nubs and winter's comin'. What else could you do?"

Again Barry studied the stranger, his look thoughtful. He reached for the Bull Durham pouch in his shirt pocket, and while he shook out the makings for a cigarette asked, "You sure you're a bronc stomper?"

"I've done a few things."

"Why aren't you workin' for Hoover anymore?"

"He asked me to leave."

"Why?"

"He found out where I was before I started workin' for him."

Barry looked up, a question on his brow. "Where was that?" he asked, deftly rolling a cigarette with thick work-stained fingers.

"Prison."

Barry's movements froze, and the room was quiet save for clinking of dishes in the kitchen. He looked levelly at the big stranger who returned his gaze unflinching. "What was you in prison for?" he asked.

"Horse stealin'."

Barry threw back his head and laughed, the sound loud and harsh in the room. Shaking his head in wonder he looked back at the stranger whose expression was unchanged. "You got a lotta gall mister," he said, half in disbelief, half in reluctant appreciation. After a brief moment of studying the man across the table he put his unlit cigarette in the corner of his mouth and said, "You're hired. Maybe I'm a fool, I don't know, but I'm interested to see how this plays out. Anyway, everything you said was true, and you're handy. There's another reason we need someone to break them horses though. The bronc stomper we had is layin' in Doc Callaghhen's office more dead than alive. Seems one of them ponies is a man-killer. Throwed young Howard down hard then near about stomped the life outa him. A big bay horse, the kind that makes you look twice, only don't bother. Next time we get him in, just shoot him and be done with it." Turning to Daniels, who'd watched the scene unfold in amazed silence, he said, "Nathan here will take you up there in the mornin'. We got them ponies up at Two Canyons line shack seein' how we're shorta graze around here."

Barry got to his feet and the big man rose with him. Daniels remained seated, still watching.

"I don't think I caught your name," Barry said.

"Sullivan. Jake Sullivan."

"Clifford Barry."

The two men shook hands, and then Barry turned to Daniels and said, "This here's Nathan Daniels. He sleeps up at the big house on accounta the fact that Abe Daniels who owns this outfit is his pa. You'll have to settle for the bunk house like the rest of us that's got to work for a livin'."

II

Jake Sullivan was up before the sun found the hazy sky over the eastern hills. He paused a moment at the bunk-house door to survey the buildings of the Anchor D. Seen in the soft light of early morning, the place had a solid, comfortable feel, and he liked it. A light showed from the kitchen window across the compound, and someone was wrestling a box from a wagon near the back door, the only movement in a yard that was otherwise sleepy and still. The air was too warm and with no dew on the ground, it promised to be another hot, oppressive day. Jake made his way to the corrals north of the barn, climbed over the top rail and swung the back gate open. Several horses grazed half way up a long gentle slope, and he saw his gelding off by himself. As he watched, one of the Anchor D horses separated itself from the herd, pinned back his ears and wheeled aggressively toward the big gray. A hint of a smile touched Jake's eyes when his horse, indifferent to the intrusion, gave no ground and continued grazing. The other horse snorted, shook his head and retreated back to the herd. Jake gave a short shrill whistle, and as his gelding's head came up, he headed for the barn to get his rig. When he stepped back outside, the gray was waiting by the door.

"Mornin', you unsociable scoundrel," Jake said as he slipped the bridle on his horse. "I see none of my charm's been rubbin' off on you. I think more likely it's the other way around."

Once the horse was saddled, Jake stood with both arms on the top rail, quiet and patient as he watched a dull red sun slowly take the shadows from the dusty compound. He could hear movement in the bunkhouse, and then he noticed the Chinese boy was struggling with a large sack in the back of the wagon. *Lee-two*, Jake thought, recalling the names he'd picked up from last night's conversation. He hesitated briefly, then climbed the fence and walked over to him. The boy's head turned sharply at his approach, and Jake wondered at the hint of panic in his eyes. He smiled what he hoped was a reassuring smile and said, "Let me give you a hand with them sacks."

The boy nodded politely, and then backed away from the wagon to regard Jake from a safe distance. Jake thought he was about to bolt for the cookhouse door, but he stood his ground, a slender youth, with unusually fine features. He wore a loose fitting threadbare coat that was several sizes too big for him and both his sleeves and pant legs were rolled up. Oddly, Jake noticed the boy's small feet, and thought they were a perfect match for his small frame.

Climbing up into the wagon box, Jake saw that it still held three, one hundred pound sacks of flour, and two fifty pound sacks of sugar. He set the smaller bags of sugar beside a flour sack on the end gate, motioned to them and said, "If you can handle these, I'll get the rest."

The boy nodded that he understood, fumbled awkwardly with the first sack, and then carried it through the door to the kitchen. Jake slid the other two flour sacks to the back of the wagon, jumped to the ground, and then heaved the first sack up onto his shoulder. He met Lee-two at the kitchen door, and the boy stepped lightly aside to let him enter, and then moved quickly outside.

It took a moment for Jake's eyes to adjust to the dimly lit room, and when he saw Lee-one standing at the cook stove, he understood. The man had a strong face, but his left arm hung useless and withered at his side, and when he walked toward Jake, he moved with a noticeable limp. It was as if the Anchor D had hired a two for one to do the work of one man. Lee-one and Lee-two were fitting names he supposed, as the boy and his father needed each other. Jake wondered if this explained the boy's uncertainty, as maybe they were afraid of being let go. Lee-one smiled and motioned to a cluttered table, where Jake deposited the sack.

"Tank you, tank you," Lee-one said, bowing ever so slightly.

"Not a problem," Jake responded stiffly.

Lee-two came in and set the last sugar sack on the table, then turned to Jake. Their eyes met briefly, and Lee-two smiled his thanks before dropping his eyes to the floor and heading to the stove where he began flipping flap-jacks.

When Jake had deposited the last flour sack onto the table, Lee-one came over carrying a steaming coffee pot with his good hand. He motioned with his head to some cups on the counter and said quickly, "Coffee? Coffee?"

"Sure. Thanks."

Jake picked out a cup that still had a handle, and when Lee-one had filled it, mumbled his thanks and stepped through the door to the eating area. He walked past a stack of dishes on the end of the table closest to the door and took a seat against the back wall, enjoying a few minutes of solitude before the first of the Anchor D riders began to filter in. Several of the hands greeted him with a polite nod, but no one took a seat beside him. Jake was just as glad, as he was uncomfortable with small talk. Lee-two brought the food in and for the most part, the crew ate in silence. About halfway through the meal, the door came open and Nathan Daniels stepped in. Jake noted a grim set to his jaw, and he seemed to be in a sour disposition. Without a word or any sign of acknowledgment he sat down beside Jake, and was soon busy eating. Then Cliff Barry got to his feet, wiped his mouth with the back of his hand, and began speaking.

"Well boys, it's like we said last night. We're gonna have to start ridin' some bigger circles. Arnie, you take your crew and comb the drainages along the Judith. Cob, I want your boys to head toward the gap and look for sign. Could be some cows drifted on over an' are scattered along the Musselshell. Some of them high country springs must still be runnin' so don't forget to swing west. Take a couple of pack horses, 'cause you'll be gone a few days. We'll be sendin' a wagon with Arnie. Any questions?"

When no one responded, Barry looked over at Daniels. "I reckon you better stay back an' help our new bronc stomper get settled. I think Howard still had plenty of grub up there, but if you think he'll run short, come on back an' fetch the other wagon."

Daniels gave Barry the briefest of nods then went back to eating. Barry watched him for a few smoldering moments and then continued speaking. "If you manage to get through that before the week's up, you might want to head north and find Arnie's crew. Just try to steer clear of Utica. You're not likely to find any strays playin' faro in Carmody's."

This time Daniels didn't acknowledge the foreman, but continued eating as if he hadn't heard a word. All conversation in the room subsided, stifled by a palpable tension, and Jake watched with interest over the brim of his coffee cup. It seemed the crew was uncomfortable with the exchange, and wanted to keep a distance as much as possible. It was obvious that Barry didn't care.

"Well, let's head 'em out," Barry said finally. "Luck to y'all."

With the scraping of chairs and the rattle of dishes all the crew filed out, leaving Daniels and Jake alone. Daniels made no effort at conversation but finished his meal in sullen silence while Jake sipped his coffee and waited. His breakfast finished, Daniels sat studying his empty plate for a few moments. Then with a heavy sigh he got to his feet.

"Well, I guess we may as well get started," he said. "Go fetch your horse and I'll meet you south of the buildings."

Jake nodded and then watched as Daniels headed out the door without looking back. After a couple of minutes Jake rose and followed him.

The ranch yard was a beehive of activity, and as Jake made for the barn someone wheeled a canvas-covered chuck wagon up behind the kitchen. Somebody had moved his horse outside the corral and a string of ponies were shuffling in at a lazy trot, kicking up a dusty haze that all but obscured the rider trailing them. It was a tired, thirsty land and the cloudless sky promised no relief. Jake met Barry coming out of the barn.

"I'll be gone for a few days, Sullivan," Barry said. "I think you'll find most everything you need up there, but make sure you take stock of what you got for grub before young Daniels leaves. If you're short he'll bring you some back. If he don't show, the useless whelp likely took a roundabout through town and you'll just have to fend for yourself."

Jake nodded. Barry made as if to go and then quickly turned back.

"One other thing," he said. "Don't mess with that big blaze-faced bay. Just put a bullet in him when you get a chance. You'll spot him easy 'cause he's a looker, and Howard marked him up a little before gettin' the worst of it. We're gonna need some ponies pretty quick too. This hot, dry weather ain't helpin' their feet any."

Again Jake nodded but said nothing. He watched as Barry turned and strode purposefully toward the bunkhouse, then he went to his horse. After watering him at the trough by the barn, he mounted up and rode to the south edge of the compound. He didn't have long to wait before Daniels showed up mounted on a likely looking buckskin. He seemed in no mood to talk, so wordlessly Jake fell in behind, letting him take the lead.

They followed a wagon trail along the creek, past a stand of cottonwoods, and then began a long gentle climb to the southwest. The hills on either side rose sun-browned and tired against a brassy sky, and ahead Jake saw a tall, grassy hill standing apart from the others, rising steeply on all sides to a rampart-like crown of tumbled boulders. Riding in silence, they skirted the base of the hill, leaving the main trail at a dry wash that spilled from a deep waterless creek bed angling in from the south. Soon they were climbing through the dappled shade of wind stunted timber. This gave way to more grassland, and here and there beneath the cottonwoods pools of slow moving water showed themselves before disappearing back into the rocky creek bottom. From the looks of the sharp banks and the deep cuts where the stream bed turned, Jake could tell there were times of the year when a lot of water moved through this little valley.

Daniels pulled his horse to a stop, so Jake did the same. He noticed the buckskin had flecks of foamy sweat on the inside of his back legs down to the hocks, but so far his own horse seemed unfazed by the heat. Daniels turned in the saddle and looked as if he was about to say something, then thought better of it. Jake waited as the horses swished their tails at the lazy drone of flies, and then young Daniels turned again and spoke.

"What did Barry have to say?"

"Not much."

"No?"

Jake paused a moment, then said, "He said to make sure we did an inventory on food supplies before you left, so if I was needin' anything you could fetch it for me."

Daniels nodded. "What do you think of an outfit where the owner's son is nothin' but an errand boy?"

Again Jake waited a moment before speaking, his horse shifting its weight from one hip to the other, and then he said, "I reckon there's been a lot of water under the bridge I know nothin' about. I ain't makin' no judgements."

Daniels looked quickly into Jake's eyes and then turned away. After a moment he said, "It's only a couple miles farther pretty little spot. I think it's my favorite place on the ranch." He put the buckskin in motion and Jake followed.

More water flowed in the stream bed and the grass along its banks seemed a little less sun scorched. Ahead of them the pine covered slopes reached down to the trail and soon they were riding in welcome shade. They were angling back west when they broke from the trees and found themselves in a long narrow basin. The creek, which was flowing freely now, took a hard bend to the south at the foot of a high rocky outcrop, and just upstream on the far side Jake could see a log cabin, a small barn, and a series of corrals. About half a mile up the slope behind the cabin, the valley forked off in two directions with a steep and narrow, flat-topped mesa forming what looked to be an impassible barrier between two narrow canyons. Jake could see well up the valley to the left but the one on the right was pretty much hidden behind the shoulder of a jagged ridge.

The trail dropped steeply to the creek, and they splashed across, then rode up the other side. Daniels dismounted and entered the cabin while Jake sat his horse and had his look around. Like the home ranch, this place had a solid, sturdy feel. Everything was well built and well cared for, showing the signs of a well-run, here-to-stay outfit. He turned back to face the cabin as Daniels came to the door. The young man pushed back his hat and stood for a moment with his hands on his hips, a slight scowl on his face. It was a good-looking face now that the morning's sulk had left it.

"We got a big mess here," he said, looking up at Jake.

The furrow in Jake's brow betrayed an unspoken question.

"I guess no one's been back since they run Corb Howard into town. Looks like he was bleedin' pretty good."

Jake stepped off his horse, dropped the reins and followed Daniels into the cabin. A swarm of flies came off a torn shirt lying crumpled on the floor, and the sheets on the unmade bed were stained a dark red going to brown. Flies flew from the bed to rattle on the window pane above a small table littered with dirty bandages and unwashed dishes.

"I guess they left in a hurry," Jake said. Daniels nodded, and Jake continued. "It's too hot to have a fire inside. I'll start one outside so we can heat some water to clean this stuff up."

"Sure. I'll see what's left for food, and then give you a hand."

Jake started the fire close to the creek so he wouldn't have far to carry the water. He found a couple of good sized kettles in the cabin, and once the water was heating, went to his horse, loosened the cinch, then found some shade under the eaves of the cabin. Daniels came out to sit beside him, took off his hat and threw it on the ground.

"You should be good for a week or so," he said. "I'll have to run up here with a wagon pretty quick though."

Jake nodded but made no reply.

"I reckon the ponies have all drifted up one of them canyons. I'll help you run 'em in before I head back."

Again Jake nodded, and then looked at the sky. "That might not be till tomorrow," he said.

"That's how I got it figured," Daniels agreed.

They sat in silence for a few minutes, and then Jake got to his feet. "I'll go check the water," he said. "I reckon she's hot by now."

By the time everything was cleaned up it was mid-afternoon. They heated up a can of beans and made a pot of coffee, and after they'd eaten, doused their fire and mounted up.

The tracks showed that the horses had headed up the right fork, and Jake was surprised when the canyon appeared to be well over two miles long. They followed a small feeder creek meandering down the valley floor at the foot of the mesa, and after climbing for about half a mile, the terrain leveled off and the grass became more plentiful. Ahead, gathered in the shade of an aspen bluff, Jake spotted several horses. They had their heads up and were watching their approach. The air was hot and still between the canyon walls, and Jake reined in and wiped the sweat from his forehead, then moved his gelding forward again. When they had ridden within two hundred yards, the loose horses ahead began to mill nervously. Jake reined in again and said quietly, "Hold up a second."

Daniels pulled up and glanced at Jake who was watching the horses intently.

"Is that him?" Jake asked, not taking his eyes from the horses.

"What's that?"

"Is that him? The horse that busted up your man?"

Daniels looked back to the horses. He could feel their nervous tension, and his own buckskin was growing restless and fidgety. "I don't know," he said. "They keep movin' and I can't tell which one you're lookin' at."

"That's okay, it don't matter. I'm sure I got him spotted. There's a few fine mares in there too. That's good. That's real good."

Daniels was surprised at the intensity in Jake's voice and he glanced his way again, remembering the man's confession that he was a horse thief.

A light came into Jake's eyes as he chuckled, "Well look at you tough fella."

Daniels looked back to the horses. A big, bald-faced chestnut had taken a few strides toward them, his neck arched and his nostrils flared as he tossed his head, pawing the air with a front hoof. His mane flashed in the late afternoon sun, and Daniels felt a thrill go through him.

"Let's swing wide to the right so they think we're goin' on' by," Jake said. "Don't even look at 'em till we're well past."

Daniels nodded.

"That big bay don't want nothin' to do with us," Jake continued. "That's him hangin' back there, always keepin' as far away from us as possible. I remember that horse. He's a looker all right."

Daniels looked, but still couldn't pick out the horse. He was intrigued, however, by Jake's comment about remembering him. *There's more to this story,* he thought.

Jake had moved out, so Daniels put his horse in motion and pulled alongside. Jake's big gelding was shuffling along at a lazy walk, and both the man and his horse appeared to be totally unconcerned. Daniels, for his part, was having a hard time getting his horse to settle down. Eventually, however, the buckskin seemed to take on the attitude of the big horse beside him and soon they were moving in a comfortable walk. Daniels looked over at Jake, and once again, was struck by the similarities between the horse and its rider. He surprised himself when he said, "If I owned that big steel gray of yours, I think I'd call him Jake." He was surprised again at the smile that broke across Jake's normally taciturn face.

"That's what he's called," Jake said. "That's his name. Big Jake. That's the reason I bought him in the first place; well, that and the fact that he's a mighty fine animal."

Daniels laughed and it felt good. He suddenly realized that he was enjoying himself more than he had in a long time. It was surprising considering how the day had started.

They were well past the horses now and Jake pulled in to a stop. "Now whatever happens," he said, "we need to cut that big bay back. Don't let him come in with the others."

"You gonna shoot him?"

Jake looked up startled, then shook his head and said, "Oh no, not a chance. I just ain't gonna make him come in. He's gonna have to want to."

Daniels nodded, but wasn't sure he understood. "Why ain't you gonna shoot him like Barry said?" he asked. "The horse is a man-killer."

Jake looked intently at Daniels and said, "Well there's a good chance Barry don't know what he's talkin' about. Anyway, if he is a man-killer he's gonna have to prove it to me. There's been a lot of water under the bridge that I don't know about, so I ain't makin' no judgements."

Daniels looked quickly into Jake's eyes, and then looked away. He wondered if Jake remembered saying that very same thing with regard to him that morning.

"I got a feelin' now that I think about it," Jake continued. "We're gonna have trouble cuttin' that fella back. He's sure enough scared of us, and he's built for speed. He'll likely be out front I'm guessin', an' if that happens, I'll have to blow by the herd an' try to turn him up the other valley. You keep the big bunch movin' and when they try to follow me, I'll turn back an' stop 'em. We should be able to keep 'em movin' down to the corrals, and that'll leave Big Bay out here all by his lonesome. Let's go."

They moved out two abreast, their horses moving in an animated trot, anticipating what lay ahead. The bald-faced chestnut had come out to face them again, and as they closed the distance, he screamed a high pitched squeal, turned and fled. The whole herd was instantly on the run, over thirty animals moving as one, flowing over the uneven ground like liquid – alive and moving. Hooves pounded on stone and behind them in a cloud of dust the two riders came on hard, their horses stretching out with the thrill of the chase. The herd began to thin out as the faster animals took the lead, and sure enough, the big bay was two lengths out front and gaining. Young Daniels looked over at Jake who had pulled off to the side, and then couldn't keep from laughing in sheer joy as he saw the big, iron gray horse level out, eating up the ground in massive strides as he blew by the tail end of the herd. He wondered if Jake had a ghost of a chance of beating the leaders to the end of the valley, and then a large deadfall loomed before him. His horse leapt it without breaking stride, but then had to fight for his footing as they immediately dropped into a ragged gully. They hit the bottom with a hail of stones and Daniels was thrown forward in the saddle, and then in two jarring driving leaps they were up and over the other side. As his horse stretched out again, Daniels peered through the dust for Jake but couldn't see him.

Jake was clear of the main herd now, with three horses still in front of him. His gelding was moving with a beautiful easy rhythm, and then he was alongside a rangy dun that veered off to the side as he pounded on past. Next he was by the big chestnut, and then there was only the bay between him and the mouth of the canyon. He reined over in behind so his horse would know he didn't want to pass, and he felt the gray pushing on his hands to let him know he wasn't happy about conceding the horse race. Ahead of him the valley widened, and then they were past the last sloping rocks of the mesa. As he had expected, the bay gelding wanted nothing more to do with the corrals ahead, so moving in a wide arcing circle, he raced around the shoulder of the hill, giving everything he had in a last ditch effort to gain the narrow valley and freedom.

Jake glanced over his shoulder and saw that, with him being out front, the rest of the herd had slowed down and he had a good hundred yards on the nearest horse. He angled hard to the right to take the second valley away from them, then slowed down to let them by. The bald faced chestnut was the first horse to round the end of the mesa, and instead of taking the open valley before him, he pinned back his ears and with a burst of speed, tried valiantly to get by Jake to follow the bay. Jake gave his horse his head and rode hard for the chestnut's shoulder. It was touch and go, but the horse gave ground, and soon the rest of the herd was following him down the wider valley to the corrals below. As he drew rein, Daniels pulled up beside him, his horse lathered up and breathing hard.

Daniels face was flushed with excitement, and he grinned at Jake and yelled, "Whoo-ee! That was a horse race!"

Jake grinned back and said, "Let's give 'em some room. They're more likely to find the gate if we ain't pressurin' 'em."

The valley ahead was fenced in a wide V that ran from the steep mountain slopes down to corrals. As they watched, the horses moved single file in a slow and tired lope, through the waiting gate to the horse pasture above the buildings. Jake glanced over his shoulder, but there was no sign of the big bay.

—〰—

They spread their bedrolls on a flat piece of ground between the corrals and the cabin, as it was too hot and stuffy inside. Beneath a blanket of stars they sipped hot black coffee, the warm glowing embers of their dying fire reflected on their faces. The comfortable silence was broken by the sound of a horse whinnying somewhere up the dark valley. An answering whinny came from just behind the barn, and Daniels looked across the fire at Jake and smiled.

"I guess he decided to pay us a visit after all," he said.

Jake smiled back. "Looks that way," he said.

III

"I almost wish I was stayin' around to see the fireworks," Daniels said moments after mounting up.

Jake was looking off up the valley where the blaze-faced bay was pacing back and forth behind a closed gate. He turned back to Daniels and said, "Oh, I don't expect there'll be too many fireworks."

"No?"

Jake shook his head.

"How do you figure that?" Daniels asked.

"I go about this sort of different," Jake said. "I just hope Barry don't show up before I have a chance to get a good start. He may not approve."

"That sound's mighty interestin'," Daniels said. "What do you do that's so different? You're gonna have to crawl up onto the middle of them ponies no matter what."

Jake nodded. "That's right," he said.

Daniels waited for more of an explanation, but when none was forthcoming he asked again, "So what do you do that's so different?"

"Too hard to explain," Jake said. "I'd have to show you. Anyway, I ain't likely to get started today. I'm gonna have to remodel them corrals a bit."

"Remodel the corrals?" Daniels shook his head and smiled. "Now you got me really curious."

Jake was looking up the valley again, watching the bay. "Do I have your permission?" he asked, turning back to face Daniels.

"For what?"

"To remodel the corrals."

"Why ask me?" Daniels said.

"You're the owner's son."

Daniels face became instantly sullen, and after a brief pause he said quietly, "A lot that's worth."

"It might be worth my job if Barry stops by and starts chewin' on my hide."

Daniels smiled in spite of himself and said, "If that happens you can tell Barry you got my permission."

"Thanks."

Daniels made as if to leave, but then turned back and asked, "What's wrong with the corrals?"

Jake waved a hand and said, "Nothin's wrong with them, I just need to make some changes."

"You'd have to show me?"

Jake nodded, and Daniels smiled, looking down at his hands cupped on top of his saddle horn. After a brief pause he said, "I was thinkin' of sendin' Lee-one out here with the grub, 'cause someone needs to head for town to check on Howard. Maybe I'll be back though."

Jake nodded and without saying goodbye, turned and walked to where his horse was waiting. Daniels watched him for a moment, then turned and rode across the creek and took the trail for the home ranch. The morning sun felt good on his face, and then he realized it was cooler this morning then it had been in ages, and the air had a different feel. Maybe they were finally in for a break in the weather. He glanced at the sky but there was not a cloud to be seen.

—⁓—

Jake was surprised at the extensive corral set up, as well as the size of the two holding fields. From the old cattle sign, he realized the Anchor D must have used the place as a gathering area before dispersing cattle to the high mountain pastures. It didn't sound like Barry had any plans to use it for the round up though, and he wondered why.

He'd left the horses in the field straight west of the corrals as he'd wanted a buffer zone between them and the lone bay. He rode towards them now, letting them run ahead of him from one end of the field to the other, back and forth again and again, always moving at a slow patient walk. It wasn't long before they began to see him as less of a threat, and soon he was able to sit his horse among them while they went back to grazing. After a time he rode back to the corrals, and only the bald-faced chestnut bothered to lift his head to watch him leave.

From there he rode to the small jingle pasture just north of the cabin. Without dismounting, he swung the gate open, then turned and rode up the slope to where the bay stood with his head over the gate. The horse trotted off a short distance as he approached, and then turned broadside to watch him, head high and nostrils flaring. Jake could see welts on his hind quarters and shoulders, and there was dried blood on his hocks.

"Mornin', pretty boy," Jake said just loud enough for the horse to hear. "You're a looker alright. Gettin' a little lonesome too, I'll bet."

Jake opened the gate and the horse stood his ground, every muscle under his sleek and shiny hide tense and ready. After throwing one more appreciative glance the horse's way, Jake turned and rode at a lazy trot back down the hill. A few moments later he heard the thunder of hooves behind him, and then the blaze-faced bay was pounding past him toward the corrals below. Jake reined to a stop and watched for a moment before turning back to close the gate.

Nathan Daniels dismounted in front of the cook shack, and after looping his reins over the hitch rail, stepped up into the shade of the awning. The ranch yard was eerily empty and still, and then he glanced up toward the big house and saw his father sitting on his stump chair on the veranda. He remembered the heated exchange of yesterday morning, and felt a brief touch of shame. He knew it was killing his father not to be able to help on the gather, and even though it was almost two years since the accident, it didn't seem to be getting any easier on him. Daniels sighed heavily, turned and pushed the door open.

"Lee-one?" he called questioningly. All was quiet, so he walked through the empty eating area to the kitchen. It too was empty, and the stove was cold. Stepping out the side door, he took a well-worn path to the little shack in a stand of cottonwoods that was home to Lee-one and his boy. Lee-one must have seen him coming, as the door swung open and he stepped outside. Daniels nodded a greeting and said, "I need to take a load of grub up Two Canyons. You don't know where the wagon got to do you?"

Lee-one nodded, "Take bofe wagon," he said. "Bofe wagon." Daniels shook his head in disbelief and Lee-one continued. Pointing north he said, "One wagon." Then pointing south he said again, "One wagon."

Daniels put his hands on his hips and pursed his lips, staring off at nothing. Turning back to Lee-one he asked, "Did Barry say when they'd be back?"

Lee-one nodded eagerly, "He say tree, maybe foe day."

Daniels nodded, thought a moment, and then said, "Lee-one, could I get you to throw together a few days' worth of food?" I'll have to take some up there with a pack horse or he's gonna run out."

Lee-one's nod was animated. "When you go?" he asked.

Daniels looked at the sky, calculating how much daylight he had left, hoping to avoid an evening alone with his father. It was no good though, so he looked back to Lee and said, "I'll leave first thing in the morning."

When Daniels had off saddled and turned his horse loose, he puttered around the tack room looking for something to kill time. He replaced a rein on an old bridle that some long forgotten hand had left behind, then tied a new honda in a broken rope that was too short to be of much use anyway. After that he stood and watched the empty yard through a fly specked window while the shadows began to lengthen. Finally he stepped outside and made the long walk up to the house on legs that were suddenly tired.

His father was still seated on his stump chair when Nathan mounted the steps. Abe Daniels was a barrel-chested man of medium height with thick short arms and beefy hands. His coarse sun-weathered face beneath stiff gray hair bore no resemblance to the finer features of his son, and was a testament to the fact that his wife had been a good looking woman. His greeting to Nathan was strained and awkward.

"Howdy, Nathan."

Nathan responded with a nod, then turned and sat heavily down on the top step.

"You get the new man settled in up at Two Canyons?"

Again Nathan nodded. "He's short on food though, and Barry sent out both wagons. I'll have to pack some up there tomorrow."

"He can't hold out till Barry gets back?"

Nathan shook his head. "I don't think so," he said.

For a while no one spoke, and then Abe said, "There's a pot of beans and some biscuits in the warming oven. I've already eaten."

Nathan rose wearily to his feet. "Thanks," he said. "I could eat, that's for sure."

As he entered the house, the toe of his boot brushed against Abe's crutch which was leaning on the door jamb, and it clattered loudly to the floor.

"Oh, sorry about that," Nathan said quickly, stooping to pick it up. He handed it back to his father and their eyes met briefly. Abe was the first to look away, and then Nathan stepped inside, the door clicking shut behind him.

I V

When Daniels rode up to the Two Canyons cabin, Jake was nowhere to be seen. Several horses were in the large holding field, and two of them had their heads up looking toward the corrals behind the barn. Curious, Daniels tied his horses to the hitching rail and went to investigate. As he climbed over the rail fence into the alleyway, he noticed that the top row of rails on the far side was missing. He could hear the rhythmic hoof beats of a horse, and when he rounded the corner of the barn he saw Jake was working a short-coupled sorrel on foot in one of the smaller pens.

Daniels climbed the fence one pen over and took a seat on the top rail where he had a good view but wouldn't disturb the proceedings. As far as he could tell, Jake was unaware of his presence. The big man was standing in the center of the pen, the coils of his catch rope in his left hand, slowly swinging a loop with his right. At first Nathan thought he was going to rope the colt, but then he realized Jake was just using the loop to keep the horse moving. Round and round the horse went, moving in a relaxed trot, the sweat on his neck and flanks showing that they'd been at it for a while. Jake shifted his position ever so slightly, and the colt turned on his hocks and began circling the pen in the opposite direction. It was then that Daniels noticed that Jake had used the missing rails to take the corners from the pen. He was wondering about this when the horse came slowly to a stop, his flanks wet and shining and his sides heaving up and down.

The sorrel turned his head to watch Jake, who was making no attempt to move him out. They stood that way, the man patient and still, and the colt with his distended nostrils moving with the rhythm of his breathing. Daniels was unsure of what he was witnessing, but he could feel a tense connection between the man and the horse, and was aware of his own heart beating. Then as he watched, the horse turned and walked over to stand head down and humble beside the man.

Daniels let out his breath, unaware that he'd been holding it. Jake was now talking in soothing tones, and he placed a big hand on the animal's forehead, held it there, and then slowly slid it off. Next he was scratching the horse behind the ears, down the neck and onto the shoulder, always speaking in a gentle re-assuring voice. Then he bent down and picked up a front foot, and to Daniels' amazement, the colt stood relaxed and unafraid. Jake walked around the horse, picking up first one foot then another, until he'd picked up all four feet. Then he was back at the colt's head, praising him in that same quiet voice. After a few moments of this, he turned and walked away and the horse followed, his face inches from Jake's back. When Jake turned the horse turned; when he stopped, the horse stopped too.

Jake continued with this for a while, pausing every now and then to give the colt a re-assuring scratch on the neck or withers. Next he led him over to a boxed-off corner, slid his saddle from underneath the rail, and unceremoniously threw it up onto the horse's back. The off stirrup came down, slapping the colt on the ribs, but he took it unconcerned. Daniels couldn't believe what he was witnessing, and his mind was full of conflicting thoughts. Surely the horse had already been started, but then he knew it hadn't. They'd trailed out the few that Howard had ridden on the same day the wagon had hauled him into town. Could they have missed this one? But then, how would Jake have known? There was no snubbing post, no frantic hooves lashing at the air, no terrified squealing. Instead the little sorrel was somehow willing putty in the big man's hands. Jake had a halter on the horse now and was snugging up the cinch. Now he had a foot in the stirrup and was swinging a leg over. There was no explosion of wild twisting fury, no mad pounding of hooves. The colt stood calm and relaxed while Jake sat easy in the saddle.

Jake's head came up and he saw Daniels for the first time. He smiled and acknowledged him with a tip of his head.

"Howdy, Nathan," he said. "I never seen you come in."

"I reckon you were busy," Daniels responded.

"Nice little horse, this one," Jake said. "They ain't always this sweet." After a pause he continued. "I'm gonna move him out here a bit, and then if you don't mind throwin' that gate open I'll see how he likes the great wide open."

"Sure," Daniels responded.

With the halter shank hanging loose from his left hand, Jake reached back with his right and slapped the horse lightly on the hindquarter while bumping his sides with his calves. At first the gelding froze up, lifting his head and stomping a hind foot, but then he took one tentative step and the bumping stopped. His head came down, and Jake reached forward and patted his neck, then waited. After a time Jake bumped the horse again and he moved forward, taking three or four steps before stopping. The process was repeated, and soon the colt was trotting willingly around the outside edge of the pen.

After several laps, Jake pushed his feet forward in the stirrups and leaned his weight well back. "Whoa, fella," he said quietly. "Whoa now. Whoa… whoa."

The horse came to a shuffling stop, and once again received a pat on the neck. Jake turned to Daniels and nodded. Daniels jumped down from his perch, walked around to the back side of the corral and swung the gate wide. He glanced over his shoulder and saw the little sorrel watching him with interest, head up and ears forward but surprisingly relaxed. He stepped out of the open gate, then backed up a few feet and waited. He could hear encouraging words from Jake, and then the gelding's head came into Daniels' line of vision. The horse froze momentarily at the gate, its nose close to the ground and its front feet braced.

"If you get the chance, Nathan, shut the gate once we're through."

"Alright."

The sorrel snorted nervously then lunged forward, and startled by its own movements broke into a bucking run. Jake let the horse have its head and soon he was leveling out into a more relaxed stride. Daniels hurried to close the gate, and then turned to see Jake and the colt making a wide circle at the far end of the holding field. The horse accelerated on the home stretch, and when he saw the gate closed before him, shortened his stride, changed leads and turned hard for the corner of the pasture closest to the other horses. He came to a jarring stop with his head over the rails, and Jake reached forward to give him a re-assuring pat on the neck. He seemed content to let the horse stand, and Daniels, remembering his own horses, headed for the cabin to unpack. By the time he had the diamond off the pack horse, Jake and the sorrel were moving in a relaxed trot along the fence at the far end of the holding field.

—⟋⟍⟍—

Daniels had the lamp lit and was just finishing up the supper dishes when Jake stepped through the door. Wordlessly, the big man went to the stove, poured himself a cup of coffee, and then took a chair at the table where he sat in taciturn silence. Daniels was getting used to Jake going long periods without speaking, but never felt the silence was because he was uncomfortable with conversation, but rather that he was comfortable with silence. Instead of being a shield to keep him away, it seemed to draw Daniels in, and Jake seemed to welcome the company. Daniels threw his dishtowel over a nail behind the stove, poured a cup of coffee and joined Jake at the table. He too found that he was comfortable with the silence, so for a while he said nothing.

There were too many questions waiting to be asked though, but instead of voicing them he said, "You're one different kind of bronc stomper, Mr. Jake Sullivan."

Jake looked at him, and then nodded. "Different than some I suppose," he agreed.

"Where'd you learn all that stuff? I still can't figure out what it is you're doin' but it's sure workin'."

"Them ponies worked good for you?"

Daniels nodded. "Considerin' they just had their first saddlin' this mornin'. That bald-faced chestnut acted plum broke."

"He's a good one all right. I hope I get the chance to put a little extra time on him."

Daniels shrugged. "When Barry sends someone up here to get horses, just don't let on that you got to him yet. They won't know the difference or take the time to ask."

Jake thought a moment, and then said, "Maybe I'll turn him out at night with the ponies I ain't saddled yet. That way they'd ask no questions and I wouldn't be tellin' no lies."

Daniels looked at Jake surprised. *He goes to prison for horse stealin' but draws the line at tellin' lies,* he thought. He shook his head, but it went unnoticed as Jake was quietly looking out the window watching the last of the day's falling light fade to darkness.

"Anyway," Daniels said, "You ain't told me where you learned to break colts like that. I've never seen anythin' like it."

Jake took a drink of his coffee, leaned forward, and placing both arms on the table said, "Most of it I learned from an old Mexican I worked for back in California, but I reckon I've been learnin' it all my life."

Daniels sat back and wrinkled his brow, "What do you mean?" he asked.

Jake's thoughts seemed far away when he responded, "The first lesson I remember, and maybe the most important one, I learned from a pretty little school marm back in the Dakotas. I was only twelve, but I was in love with her and figured sure I'd marry her one day."

"Lucky you," Daniels said. "My school teacher was old, fat an' ugly, an' liked nothin' better than to whack me over the head with her yard stick. I figured sure I'd murder her one day."

"I had one like that too," Jake said seriously. "Only he was a man and preferred a leather strap. I was never any good at spellin' and he figured a few good licks on my hand would cure that. It didn't work but he kept tryin'. I was never so happy as when he took sick and got replaced by Miss Peterson. Anyway, it didn't take her no time at all to figure out I couldn't spell, an' one day when she let the other kids out for recess, she told me I had to stay behind. I figured I had another strap comin' but I didn't mind so much 'cause I figured she wouldn't be able to hit near so hard as Mr. Harmon. Besides, I'd already fallen in love with her, and there was no one in the world I'd rather get the strap from. Instead of givin' me a strap though, she says, "Jake, I want you to give me a spellin' test. I'll tell you a word, and then I'll write it on the blackboard. You take a piece of chalk and mark it right or wrong. If I make any mistakes, I want you to correct me." Well she'd say a word, and then spell it out on the board, an' most of the time she'd spell it right. Every once in a while she'd spell a word wrong though, and usually in a funny way that would make me laugh. Then I'd write it out proper for her. About the fifth time I corrected her she stood back and smiled at me and said, "Well look at you, Jake Sullivan. You know how to spell after all. You just thought you couldn't." From then on I was a pretty fair speller, and more in love with her than ever. What Miss Peterson taught me was that it's hard to learn anythin' if you're scared to death. I reckon the same goes for most people, dogs, horses an' the rest of God's critters."

Jake finished speaking, and Daniels was silent for a few moments, then he laughed.

"What?" Jake asked.

"I worked with you all afternoon an' I never heard you string more 'n three words together. Now you're waxin' eloquent."

Jake smiled and nodded. "I can't help it," he said. "It always happens when I think about Miss Peterson."

Daniels laughed again. "What ever happened to her?" he asked.

"Mr. Harmon got better an' she left. I ran away, lied about my age and joined the Pony Express."

Daniels looked at him disbelieving. "Musta been before you hit your growth spurt," he said.

"I didn't last too long, that's a fact." Jake got up and went to the stove. "Can I pour you some more coffee?" he asked.

"Sure, thanks. I see you're keepin' the man-killer shut up in the horse pasture with your gelding."

"That's right. I'm hopin' some of Big Jake's manners rub off on him."

"What do you mean?" Daniels asked.

Jake took his seat at the table again. "Big Jake likes me. He comes when I call, and even if I don't call he takes an interest in what I'm doin'. That pretty bay'll pick up on that and start to have an attitude adjustment without even knowin' its happenin'."

"Makes sense I guess," Daniels said thoughtfully. "You think it'll make much of a difference?"

"I hope so," Jake said. "There's a fair bit of erasin' needs to happen first."

Both men sat in silence for a while, and outside a coyote began yapping at the night. Presently Jake broke the silence. "I never met your pa when I was at the ranch," he said.

Daniels sighed heavily, shifted uncomfortably in his chair then said, "No, he don't get out of the house much. His horse hit a dog hole an' fell on him a couple of years back an' he's pretty crippled up."

"You an' him don't see eye to eye I reckon."

Daniels didn't respond right away. Then staring at the table he said softly, "Ma checked out when I checked in. I don't think he ever forgave me."

V

The bald-faced chestnut took the steep downgrade willingly enough, and by the time they reached the bottom they were accompanied by the rattling of loose stones. The gelding had a good sweat on, and the afternoon's ride had done a lot to point him in the direction of being a broke horse. Jake had ridden up the right fork of the two canyons and managed to find a rough and broken trail to the rim. There he'd struck south along a timbered ridge that was sometimes wide and sometimes narrow, past the slopes of the mesa that separated the two valleys. Jake was surprised at how much country he'd had to cover before breaking out of the trees to look for a way down into the second canyon. He was also surprised when he'd found a fair bit of fresh cow sign on the cap rock above the canyon, along with some older sun dried cow pies. With the afternoon all but spent, he'd decided not to investigate, but to tell Daniels about it next time he was out.

Jake was almost to the canyon mouth when his gelding's head came up. He heard a hoof on stone, and then a rider came into view around the shoulder of the mesa, coming down the valley Jake had climbed earlier in the afternoon. It was Cliff Barry, and his trail gaunt horse was favoring a front foot. Barry nodded a greeting as he approached, and then drew rein.

"Howdy," he said, and Jake could tell he was as worn down as his horse.

Jake returned the greeting with a nod of his own, and when his eyes went to the left front foot of Barry's horse, Barry said, "Threw a shoe a couple hours back. I've been combin' the high country since I left Cob's wagon over on the Musselshell yesterday mornin'." Turning in the saddle, Barry motioned with his arm to the ridge Jake had just come off of and continued speaking. "I followed that ridge there, then found my way down the canyon. Not a single cow. Not even any sign. We're havin' a rough time of it, Sullivan."

Jake nodded again, and hoped the surprise he felt didn't show in his face. Barry had lied, and he wondered why. If he'd followed the ridge like he said he had, he couldn't help but have seen the cattle sign. Not only that, but they almost surely would have met up. Then a thought came to him. Maybe Barry had dropped down on the far side of the ridge in an effort to cover more country, and had missed seeing the sign and running into him because of it. Without wanting to appear too interested Jake asked, "How 'bout on the other side of the ridge? Did you look down that way?"

Barry didn't seem to think the question strange, but just shook his head. "No," he said. "My horse was too played out. Nothin' in the way of grass over there anyway. Mostly just heavy timber."

Jake nodded and looked away. He had no idea why Barry was lying, but caution told him he'd best not say anything about being up on the ridge or the cattle sign he'd seen. Barry was studying his horse.

"Say, that's one of them colts ain't it. He's sure comin' along fine."

"He's a good one," Jake acknowledged. "I think young Daniels has his eye on him."

Barry's head came up sharply. "Has he been up here?" he asked.

Jake nodded. "For a few days. He just headed back to the ranch yesterday 'cause we're runnin' low on grub." Jake could tell Barry wasn't pleased, but he waited for him to speak.

Barry chewed on his bottom lip for a while, then looked at him and said, "I hope the useless whelp wasn't in your way."

Jake shook his head. "No. He's good with the horses."

Barry rolled his eyes. "There's a first," he said. "Anyway, I didn't hire two bronc stompers. Next time he shows up send him packin'. We got too much to do for him to waste his time up here." Barry kicked his tired horse into motion, heading for the canyon mouth, and Jake fell in behind. When they'd ridden a few hundred yards Barry reined in and turned around.

"I reckon I'll be bunkin' in with you tonight. In the mornin' we'll swap ponies seein' how you got that one shod. Mine could use the rest, an' anyway, he'll likely be sore footed for a few days. Maybe throw on another shoe and do a re-set when you got the time."

Jake nodded, and once again fell in behind as they headed for the cabin below. He wondered if Barry would notice the blaze face bay in the horse pasture with his gelding, but he seemed pre-occupied and rode straight to the barn without so much as a sideways glance.

Both men dismounted, and as Barry flipped his stirrup up over his saddle he said, "Sullivan, there's no need for you to be puttin' a polish on these colts. Just get the edge knocked off 'em and the boys'll do the rest. They'll soon get enough miles on 'em without you havin' to do it."

"I don't mind," Jake said. "I got my way of doin' things and I'm makin' good progress."

Barry paused before pulling off his saddle, and looking over his horse's back, said firmly, "Well I got my way of doin' things and you're workin' for me. I want you stickin' close to the buildin's so when I send a man up here to fetch some horses you'll be handy to help drive 'em back to the home place. I can't afford to have someone waitin' around while you're off in the hills gallivantin'."

Barry pulled his rig off his horse and turned for the barn without waiting for a reply. Jake watched him go, and then turned to take off his own rig, his mind full of questions. Something about the man got his hackles up, and maybe it was just his own stubborn pride, not liking to be told how to do his job. He remembered the cow sign up on the ridge though, and couldn't help feeling something was not right. He should probably just forget about it and do the job he'd been hired to do, he reasoned. What difference did it make to him anyway? He met Barry coming out of the barn door and stepped aside.

"I'm near about starved," Barry said. "I think I'll head inside and find somethin' to eat."

Jake nodded. "I'll start pullin' them shoes," he said.

Jake threw his saddle over a rail, and then went to the corner of the barn to get a large tin pail that held the shoeing tools. He stepped outside and went to Barry's gelding, pausing briefly before bending to pick up the right front foot. He was about to reach for the nippers when his movements froze momentarily. Fresh cow manure was packed under the rim of the shoe and next to the frog. Barry had most definitely seen the cattle sign, and for some reason he didn't want him to know about it. Then Jake noticed something else. The gelding had dried mud stuck to the hair on all four feet, and it went well above the fetlocks. Where had Barry managed to find wet enough ground to sink a horse in a country that was bone dry and thirsting for rain? Jake glanced toward the cabin, and then busied himself with pulling the shoe. He didn't want to give Barry any reason to believe he'd been caught in his lie, but no matter what Barry said about sticking close to the buildings, Jake decided he'd go have his look around.

Barry rode out early in the red light of an ominous sunrise. The air was pregnant with silence, and Jake could hear the foot falls of Barry's horse long after he'd crossed the creek. He caught his gelding and led him to the pen where he'd been starting the colts, leaving the gate to the alley open so the blaze-faced bay could follow him in if he chose to, then went to the barn for his rig. As he was stepping back into daylight, he heard the bay whinny anxiously as he ran down the alley into the waiting pen. Jake smiled, set his saddle down and strolled over to close the gate behind him.

He spent the early part of the morning working the bay much as he had the other horses, only this time he did it from the back of Big Jake. At first the colt was terrified, pounding hard around the outside of the corral looking for a way out. Jake's horse had become his source of security over the past while, however, so he had conflicting emotions. It wasn't long before the bay had an ear cocked toward Jake and was no longer in flight mode. By late morning he was haltered and jogging in step with Jake's gray as Jake rode up the slope through the top gate.

Jake reached the mouth of the two canyons and glanced uneasily at the mesa rim far above. Something wasn't right and he couldn't shake the nagging feeling. The smell of dust and scorched grass clung to the air, oddly vivid and alive. He moved reluctantly forward, taking the trail that led up the left fork, and then was surprised by the low distant rumble of thunder. He glanced at the sky overhead, but what little he could see above the canyon rim showed no trace of clouds. He stubbornly pressed on, picking his way around shrubs and boulders as he made the long steady climb. The valley grew narrow and the bay colt began to pull on his lead shank. Again Jake heard the rumble of thunder, and a cool breeze coming down the canyon stirred up a whirling dust devil.

Jake reined in and threw another glance skyward. The blue was taking on an odd sickly green hue, and the land around was washed in a weird relief of light that made everything stand out stark and clear. A cold gust of wind started Jake's scarf snapping, and without hesitation he reined hard around and headed for home. The temperature was falling at an alarming rate, and Jake coaxed more speed from his gelding as eerie fingers of clouds tumbled over the mesa rim. Soon a solid ceiling of gray shut out the sky.

With a growing wind at their backs the horses were eager to travel, but even so, they hadn't made the canyon's mouth before the first heavy drops of rain began to fall. The even rhythm of the horse's hooves was a steady sound, and then the air was ripped apart by a hard crashing slap of thunder. Instantly the bottom fell out of the sky. Sheets of rain driven by the wind fell like a heavy curtain, all but taking the light from the day.

Jake was soaked to the skin and when he hit the grassy slopes, the buildings below were lost from sight. Mad rivers of muddy water raced him down the hill, and as he neared the cabin he could hear the steady roar from the creek that was now a river in full flood. He dismounted in front of the barn, and then movement on the far bank caught his attention. A wagon was on the steep descent to the river, and the driver, who he assumed was Daniels, was frantically trying to urge the frightened team across. Jake glanced in stark fear at the crashing foaming water, dropped his reins and lead shank, and in a slipping, sliding run raced down the greasy bank toward the raging torrent.

"Stay back! Stay back! Don't come across!" Jake waved his arms wildly, and the wagon driver straightened up and looked across the water. It was Lee-two!

"Go back! Go back!"

Lee-two hesitated, and Jake was sure he couldn't hear him.

"Go back!" he yelled again, gesturing frantically.

Lee-two was standing straight up in the wagon, and Jake felt a wave of relief when the boy turned and looked behind him.

FLASH! WHAM!

A blinding bolt of lightning shattered a cottonwood on the ridge behind Lee-two as a deafening concussion shook the ground. Jake staggered back and almost lost his footing as the terrified team lunged into their collars. The wagon jolted into motion and Lee-two fell backward over the seat, losing hold of the lines as the horses, wild with fear, plunged headlong into the boiling water. There was no turning back as they buck-jumped their way forward through the churning current. The wagon was in the water now; it teetered, and then came back down on four wheels and for a moment it looked like they were going to make it.

The wagon box was for the most part staying clear of the fast moving water, and Jake found himself shouting, "God help 'em! Please God! Come on boys! Pull now! Pull!

The team was almost across; digging and clawing they were fighting their way up and out of the water when the wagon's right front wheel dropped into a hole. Instantly the wagon was slammed sideways by the force of the raging current, and Jake had one brief glimpse of Lee-two's horror stricken face peering over the edge of the wagon box before it went over on its side. Miraculously, the horses kept their feet long enough to drag the capsized wagon almost clear of the water before they went down in a tangle of harness and thrashing hooves. Jake was scrambling over the wagon box even before it skidded to a stop, but when he looked inside, Lee-two was gone! He fought down the panic that gripped his chest and turning, looked downstream. Almost without hope, he staggered drunkenly along the bank, his wet clothes weighing him down and his feet like lead in the sucking mud. He went to his knees, fought to his feet again, and then above the roar of the river he heard it. In clear and perfect English, Lee-two was screaming.

"Help! Please help me! Help!"

At first Jake couldn't see him, but then where the river undercut the bank making a sharp turn, he saw Lee-two's head above the crashing water. He had his arm around some exposed roots, and when he saw Jake he began to scream more frantically.

"Help! Help me please! I cannot hold on!"

"I see you Lee-two! Hold on, I'm coming!"

In a stumbling run Jake made his way along the bank, and for a while Lee-two was lost from sight. When he got to the where the river turned and peered over the edge, he was relieved to find him still there. When the boy looked up at him, hope came alive in his eyes. Jake realized immediately, however, that he would be unable to reach him, and he called down, "Can you hold on Lee-two?!"

The boy nodded.

"Don't be afraid!" Jake shouted. "I have to go get a rope! I'll be right back!"

Lee-two looked directly into Jake's eyes, and again he bravely nodded.

Jake hesitated just a moment, then pulled back from the river, and with his face to the driving rain, ran back to the buildings. The team was lying still now, having stopped their fighting. The near horse, half on top of the other, lifted its head and eyed Jake as he approached, made a couple of feeble attempts to rise, and then lay back down defeated. Jake's gelding and the bay were standing head down and tails to the wind, patiently waiting at the barn door. The bay eyed him warily, but made no attempt to bolt as he went to his saddle and took down his rope.

Hurrying back to Lee-two, he gave the boy a wave in an effort to offer encouragement. Lee-two nodded slightly, but his face was strained and his eyes were flat and lifeless. Jake sensed that he couldn't hold out much longer, and a renewed sense of urgency spurred him on. With fingers clumsy with the cold, he tied his rope to the very tree whose exposed roots were Lee-two's lifeline, then throwing his hat on the bank, took a firm grip and plunged feet first into raging water a few feet upstream. The shock of the cold and the current hit him like a load of bricks, and he was slammed into Lee-two. The force of the blow was too much for the weakened boy, and with a heartbreaking cry, he lost his grip on the tree roots. Jake felt his own grip on the rope slipping as he franticly reached out for Lee-two. He caught hold of the boy's coat collar and then his head went under. Coughing and sputtering, he resurfaced, desperately trying to keep his hold while Lee-two's claw-like fingers gripped his shirt sleeve. He could feel the boy's coat was slipping off, and he knew he was losing him, but he didn't have the strength to draw him in against the force of the current. Loosening his own grip on the rope, he let the river take him, and in that moment was able to pull Lee-two against his chest. As his arm encircled Lee-two's throat, the panic stricken boy's flailing arms beat against Jake's head, and his fingers clawed his face before taking a vice like grip on his shirt collar. This gave Jake a chance to try for a better hold.

Lee-two's heavy coat was half way off as Jake reached to get his arm under the boy's arm and around his chest. As he did so, his big hand came down squarely and firmly on what was obviously a woman's breast beneath a wet shirt! *Lee-two was a girl!* In spite of the circumstances, Jake pulled his hand back as if he'd been burned, and he felt Lee-two begin to slip away. Her coat was gone now, and he fought for another hold, knowing he didn't have the luxury to worry about where his hands landed, and then he was finally holding Lee-two firmly against him. Jake shook his head and then glanced at her face, but all he saw was hope in her eyes, and he wondered if she even knew what had just happened.

"It's alright, Lee-two!" he shouted above the roar of the water. "Don't be afraid! I won't let you go!"

Lee-two nodded.

"Help me hold on, okay? I'm going to tie us together!"

Again Lee-two nodded, and she tightened her grip around his neck. The cold was quickly sucking the strength from Jake's body, and he knew he had to hurry. With arms like lead and with lifeless fingers, he passed the rope under Lee-two's arms, making two wraps before tying off. He then pushed his left arm through the loops and reached to grab the taught end of the rope. With an iron will and praying for strength, he worked his way hand over hand toward the bank. When he reached it, he was still waist deep in water, but he managed to dig his feet into the gravelly slope. He pulled his head up even with the top of the bank, but could go no further. He was so exhausted he almost didn't have the energy to care if he fell back into the water and drowned. He stood teetering, and he felt his grip on the rope slipping.

"Lee-two," he said, though his lungs could hardly find the air to make a sound. She was looking at him, and he knew she'd heard. "I'm gonna pull my arm out of the rope. You're gonna have to use me as a ladder to climb out. Can you do it?"

Lee-two nodded.

Jake pulled his arm free, then gripping the rope with both hands where it came over the bank, braced himself as much as possible. Lee-two worked her way around to his back, and then crawled and clawed her way up and over. Jake's mind was slow and dumb, and it was a moment before he realized she had made it, and he almost forgot he still had something to do. He felt Lee-two grip his shirt collar, and when he looked up her face was inches from his.

With Lee-two gripping and pulling and his dead limbs flailing, Jake somehow managed to drag himself over the lip of the bank and onto the grass. He lay for a moment with the rain on his back, then struggled to his knees but could go no further. He hung his head while his heart hammered in his chest, and then he realized he was staring stupidly at his hat which lay crushed on the wet grass. He reached for it, roughly knocked the crown back into shape, pulled it down firmly on his head and then got to his feet. Ragged and wet Lee-two stood watching him as he swayed unsteadily.

"Thank you, Mr. Sullivan," she said.

Jake didn't know why he did it, but he reached for her and she came into his arms and then she was sobbing uncontrollably, her face against his chest. Jake held her for what seemed like a long time, then not knowing where he found the strength, he scooped her up in his arms and carried her to the cabin.

VI

Jake stepped over the sill and set Lee-two down. It was unnaturally dark inside the cabin, and the cold rain rattled on the roof and window panes. Lee-two stepped back and looked uncertainly at Jake, who felt suddenly awkward. She had her arms hugged to her chest and was shivering violently.

"Why don't you grab one of them wool blankets off the bed there, Lee-two. I'll get the fire built up and then you can cozy up to the stove. I still gotta deal with them horses outside."

Lee-two nodded mutely, turned and walked over to the bed. Jake lifted the lid on the stove and was relieved to find there was still a good bed of coals. He grabbed some wood by the door and soon there was the pleasant sound of crackling pine while orange light danced on his face and on the ceiling. He closed the lid, lit a lantern, and then turned to Lee-two.

"Pull that chair up close here," he said. "It'll soon be throwin' some good heat. I'll find you a dry shirt to put on."

Lee-two looked at him timidly, and then obediently pulled her chair close to the fire. Jake found a change of clothes for himself and a wool shirt for Lee-two. He walked over to stand beside her.

"Lee-two?"

She looked up at him, and speaking gently he continued.

"I know you're a girl, and I know you speak good English. I have no idea why you feel like you gotta hide that from people, but I reckon that's none of my business. However, you're gonna be stuck here with me till the flood dies down, but you got no need to be afraid. I would never hurt you, and when this is over I won't give away your secret."

Lee-two looked at Jake with eyes open and honest, betraying a childlike trust. "I'm not afraid," she said. "I know you are a good man, Mr. Sullivan."

Jake looked quickly away, but felt strangely grateful for her comment, and then he continued speaking. "I'll be sleepin' in the barn loft an' you can have the cabin. You're gonna have to get out of them wet clothes, so for the time bein' you'll have to wear this here shirt. It'll be way too big, but it's the best I can do. You can keep a blanket wrapped around you till your clothes are dry. I won't ever come in here without knockin' first."

Lee-two reached up and took the shirt. "Thank you, Mr. Sullivan," she said. Her bottom lip began to tremble and she looked away. "I thought I was going to die," she whispered.

Jake stood and watched her, unsure what to do. Finally he said, "You're a brave girl, Lee-two," then turned and stepped outside.

The rain was still slanting in cold and hard, but there was no longer any sound of thunder. Jake splashed across the yard to the barn in a sprinting run, and once inside left the door open so he'd have light to see by. His big gray nickered at him expectantly, and the bay watched him with his ears up. Though he was shivering uncontrollably, Jake took a moment to throw a forkful of hay through the door, and the two horses began eating eagerly. By the time he'd stripped down and put on his dry clothes, his hands were shaking so hard he could hardly manage the buttons on his shirt. It was all he could do to pull on his wet boots over his dry socks, but the exertion served to warm him up a little. He took his oilskin from a hook by the door and as he shrugged into it, contemplated his next move. He realized the down team was his first priority and his saddle couldn't get any wetter, so with a sense of foreboding, he stepped out the door and slogged over to where they lay. He approached them on the up-hill side to avoid their hooves should they renew their thrashing, but save for the ribs of the near horse rising and falling, they remained still.

"Easy, boys, easy. What kind of a mess have we got here?"

Jake squatted by their heads and continued his sooth-ing talk while he scratched their necks and the side of their faces. He wondered if he should feel for broken legs, but then decided that would put him in too vulnerable a position. He'd know soon enough anyway.

He got to his feet, and then went to look in the over-turned wagon box. Surprisingly enough, there was still a jumbled mess of groceries inside, and most of it was out of the weather. Half buried beneath the pile he saw what he was looking for; a small canvas tarp that had been used to cover the load. He grabbed hold of a corner and was able to wrestle it clear, then went back to the horses. Speaking gently to re-assure them, he spread the tarp over their heads, then went back to unhook the tugs from the eveners. He was only able to unhook the yoke on the top horse, and then he slowly pulled the tarp from his head.

"Easy there fella, easy now." Jake unsnapped the lines from the horse's bit, then grabbed hold of the cheek piece on the bridle and pulled the horses head up. "Come on, fella, up you get. You can do it, on your feet now."

The horse shook his head, then with a great effort, got his front legs out in front of him and heaved himself to his feet. He snorted and shook his mane, putting no weight on his off hind foot. All at once the horse that had been buried made to rise, and Jake scrambled around in front to take hold of his bridle.

"Easy boy, easy now," Jake said, trying to reach the snap on the yoke.

The horse found his feet and lurched forward, dragging Jake along while he clung to the bridle and pulled in jerking motions on the driving line.

"Whoa now! Whoa big fella!"

Snorting loudly, the gelding came to a fidgety stop, and Jake was able to back him up enough to take the pressure off the yoke and get it unhooked. As soon as it fell away, the horse bolted for the barn with the lines trailing, while the lame horse hobbled awkwardly up the hill to join him. Jake was relieved to see he was bearing some weight on his injured leg, and he was hopeful it wasn't too serious. Stooping, he picked up the tarp, and after he'd thrown it over the groceries, he trudged wearily up to the barn. The horses stood in a tight group while he unharnessed and off saddled, and when he led his gelding to the horse pasture, the others followed submissively, heads down and single file, the limping draft horse bringing up the rear. Jake closed the gate and hurried for the dry warmth of the cabin, took hold of the door knob, and then remembered. Before he could knock, however, the door swung open before him. Lee-two was standing in the doorway wrapped snuggly in a wool blanket, the sagging sleeves of Jake's shirt rolled up to reveal her small hands.

"I was watching for you," she said. "You must be terribly cold."

Jake smiled hesitantly and stepped inside. Removing his hat he said, "At least I'm dry now for the most part."

Lee-two closed the door behind him, and Jake became aware of the sound of bacon sizzling in a pan on the stove. The pleasant smell instantly woke up his appetite, and then mingled with the aroma of frying bacon he caught the smell of coffee.

"It's your turn to warm up by the stove," Lee-two said. "Take off your wet coat and I'll get you a blanket."

Jake nodded obediently, surprised at how freely Lee-two was speaking. When he'd hung up his oilskin, he turned to find her waiting with the blanket. She motioned to the chair by the stove, and when he'd taken his seat, she draped the blanket over his shoulders.

"Thanks," he said, turning to face her. "I ain't been fussed over like this since Ma kept me home from school with the measles."

A worried look crossed Lee-two's face and she said, "I'm sorry, I hope you don't mind."

Jake shook his head. "No, ma'am I don't mind. You're gonna spoil me, that's all."

Jake moved his wet boots closer to the stove and felt the warmth of the room begin to take the chill from his bones. Lee-two came over to stir the bacon, and as Jake saw her profile framed against the dim light of the window, he wondered how, even with her hair cut short, anyone could mistake her for a boy. Her large brown eyes were deep and dark, framed by long dark lashes. Her skin was clear and smooth, and all her features, from her cheekbones to her nose and her chin were small and refined. Her mouth was small too, but her lips were full, pursed slightly outward now in concentration. She turned and caught him watching her, smiled uncertainly, then turned quickly to take a coffee cup from a hook on the wall. She filled it from the pot on the stove, and when she handed it to him he thanked her.

"Your pa's gonna be worried ain't he," he said.

Lee-two nodded soberly. "He will be terribly distressed," she said. "I do not know what I can do about it though. It shamed him that he had to send me. He cannot drive a team because of his injured arm."

Jake hadn't yet taken a drink of his coffee, but was content to wrap his cold hands around the warm cup. "How come you had to bring the wagon?" he asked. "I thought Daniels was going to do it."

"Mr. Barry did not want him too. He sent him to town to check on the injured man."

"He didn't want him too? Did he say why?"

Lee-two shook her head. "Nathan was very angry though."

Jake sat in silence for a while, sipping his coffee and mulling over what Lee-two had said. There were a lot of things about Barry and the Anchor D that made no sense, and he found himself wishing he would have made the ridge before the storm.

"The food is ready," Lee-two said.

Jake turned to regard her. "Thanks, Lee-two, I sure didn't expect you to make my supper."

"It is my job, remember?"

Jake got to his feet and shook his head. "I think after what you've been through you could expect a night off," he said. He took the seat opposite her at the table, which held a pot of steaming beans along with the bacon and the coffee pot. As he picked up his fork, Lee-two folded her hands and bowed her head. Jake quickly set his fork back down, and hearing it, Lee-two looked up.

"You do not give thanks before you eat?" she asked innocently.

"Sometimes," Jake said. "Probably not often enough I reckon."

"I saw your Bible by the bed. It looks well used."

Jake smiled, shook his head and said in a not unkind voice, "You do talk a lot once you get started don't you."

"I am sorry, Mr. Sullivan," Lee-two said quickly, looking down at the table.

"No. I'm sorry, Lee-two," Jake responded. "I didn't mean I don't like it when you talk. Anyway I reckon you're makin' up for lost time."

Lee-two smiled weakly. "I think you are probably right," she said. Then looking back at Jake she continued. "It is strange you know, for so long I have been afraid of someone finding out, and now that it has happened, it is such a relief."

Jake nodded that he understood. He wanted to ask her why she was pretending to be a boy, but instead he just looked at the bacon and said, "The foods gettin' cold and I'm powerful hungry. I'll give thanks okay? I reckon we got a lot to give thanks for."

Lee-two smiled, and Jake folded his big hands, closed his eyes and prayed.

"Heavenly Father. Thank you that you brought us safe through this day. Thanks that none of them horses broke a leg, and thanks for the food we are about to receive. Amen."

Jake paused a moment, then as he reached for his fork, Lee-two said, "I want to pray for my father."

Jake nodded and folded his hands again.

"Lord Jesus, please watch over my father. Help him to trust that I am in your care no matter what happens. Help him not to be afraid. Lord Jesus, I pray too that you would bless Mr. Sullivan. Thank you that he was willing to risk his life for a Chinese boy. Amen."

Jake sat silent for a few moments. Then after Lee-two had filled her plate he reached for his fork a third time. As he dished his beans he said, "I rode pony express for about six months when I was a youngster. Mr. Majors, who ran the outfit, made sure each of us boys had a good pistol and a Bible. I lost the pistol in a card game a long time ago. I've made good use of the Bible though."

Lee-two smiled at him and they ate the rest of the meal in silence. When Jake had finished he reached for the coffee pot, topped up Lee-two's cup and then filled his own. He made as if to speak, hesitated, then decided against it and took a drink of coffee.

"You were going to say something?" Lee-two asked.

Jake shook his head. "No. Well I mean yes, but that's okay, it's none of my business I reckon."

"You want to know why I pretend not to speak English, and why I pretend to be a boy."

Jake looked up at her, a question in his eyes. "Why do you?" he asked.

"If you answer my question maybe I will answer yours."

Jake laughed. "What kind of a deal is that?" he asked. "What do you mean, maybe you'll answer mine?"

"Maybe I want to know if you can be trusted," Lee-two said.

Jake thought about it a moment, then said, "Fair enough I suppose. But if I got to give something first, how do I know *you* can be trusted?"

Lee-two smiled a disarming smile and said, "I do not think a man like you has too much to fear from a little Chinese girl."

Jake smiled, shook his head and then looked straight into Lee-two's eyes. "Maybe I did like you better when you couldn't talk," he said. Lee-two smiled back and Jake continued, "Okay, fire away. What's your question?"

Without a moment's hesitation Lee-two asked, "Why did you steal those horses?"

The question surprised Jake, and he leaned back in his chair studying Lee-two, who returned his gaze, unflinching.

"Now how did you know about that?" he asked.

Lee-two shrugged her shoulders. "I know about a lot of things. Mr. Barry and the other men think that when a Chinese boy's mouth does not work, his ears do not work either."

Jake didn't say anything, but continued watching Lee-two, a trace of a smile in his eyes. Lee-two leaned forward putting both elbows on the table, cupped her chin in her hands and waited.

Jake sighed, straightened in his chair, and placing his cup on the table said, "You're quite a girl, Lee-two. I bet you always get your way with your pa, don't you."

Lee-two shrugged her shoulders again and said, "My way and my father's way are usually the same."

Jake smiled at her, and then his eyes became thoughtful. He looked down at his hands on the table, and then said in a quiet voice, "I was keepin' a promise."

"Keeping a promise?"

Jake looked up and nodded. "When I stole them horses."

"I do not understand."

Jake turned sideways in his chair and stretched out his legs while he leaned against the wall. He looked up at the ceiling, then back to Lee-two.

"I worked for an old Mexican on a ramshackle place in California. He was no good with money or business, but he was the best horseman I ever met. Best friend I ever had too. He'd spent most of his life raisin' and breedin' horses till he had the finest little string anyone could ever want. Trouble is, he'd made some bad business deals and owed a lot of money to a fella who was a good hater – a Mr. Morgan Foster. He was the big man in them parts an' used to getting things his way. It really went bad when one of Emilio's horses with a skinny Mexican kid ridin' him beat this fella's prize thoroughbred an' fancy eastern jockey by about six lengths at the Fourth of July horse race. Emilio bragged it up some, an' claimed any one of his horses could out run Foster's crowbait thoroughbred. Well that didn't sit too good, and not long after that, Foster demanded Emilio pay up. Of course he couldn't, so Foster moved in an' kicked us off the place. As we was leavin', Foster took great pleasure in tellin' Emilio how he was gonna shoot all them worthless mares and geld his prize stud horse. It just about killed the old man to hear it, an' anyway, I promised him I wouldn't let it happen. He also made me promise to look out for them horses after he was gone."

"You think he would have done it?" Lee-two asked incredulously. "Would that man have killed those horses?"

Jake nodded. "You bet he would. Anyway I never gave him the chance. That very night I chased them horses way out into the desert where I picked up a bunch of Emilio's Mexican friends. Three days later we had them ponies scattered so far an' wide Foster never had a hope of pickin' them up. I shoulda stayed away, but I wanted to see Emilio, and when I come back there was a warrant out for my arrest and I was sent to prison."

"What happened to your friend?"

"He died while they had me locked up. I never saw him again."

Lee-two sat silently, her face reflective. Then she looked at Jake and said. "But you kept your promise."

Jake nodded. "I'm still keepin' it too I reckon."

Lee-two looked at him questioningly.

"When I got out I did some snoopin' around. Turns out Emilio's stud and most of his mares ended up on a horse ranch near Miles City. When things didn't work out for me there, I followed some of them here."

Lee-two looked at him surprised. "You mean those horses outside are some of Emilio's?"

Jake shook his head. "No, not exactly," he said. Then with deep feeling he continued, "Every one of them's got the blood in their veins though."

No one said anything for a while. It was now completely dark outside, and the rain's steady rhythm on the roof along with the churning sound of the river was almost soothing. Jake got up to put more wood on the fire, then turned to Lee-two and asked, "What about you? What's your story?"

Lee-two didn't answer, waiting for Jake to come back to the table. As he stooped to pick up a piece of wood, however, something out the front window caught his attention.

"What in the world?" he exclaimed.

"What is it?" Lee-two asked.

"There's someone coming up the trail on the other side of the river."

Lee-two's chair scrapped on the floor and she scrambled to her feet to hurry to the window. As they watched, a lantern carried by the indistinct shadowy figure of a man came bobbing slowly down the steep bank toward them. At the river's edge the man stopped, and as he raised the lantern head high his face became visible in its light.

"It is my Father!" Lee-two exclaimed.

In a moment she was out the door, slipping and sliding down the muddy bank toward the river, her short and hurried steps made awkward by the wool blanket wrapped tightly around her slender frame. She was calling franticly in her native tongue against the sound of the mighty water, and as Jake watched, the man on the far bank leaned his head forward, and then fell to his knees. Setting his lantern on the ground, he raised his face and one good arm to the sky, and Jake could faintly hear his wailing over the roar of the river.

Jake turned quickly and took down the lantern. He put on his hat and grabbed his oilskin, then followed Lee-two down the hill. Lee-one was on his feet now, and he and his daughter were calling back and forth to one another across the crashing river. Jake could not understand a word, but the passion in their voices was unmistakable. He stepped hesitantly up behind Lee-two, and then draped his slicker over her shoulders. As he handed her the lantern, he wondered if the diamonds on her cheeks were from her tears or the rain, and then he stepped back into the shadows. He stood there, not wanting to infringe on this private family moment, but still feeling wrong about leaving Lee-two alone. His shoulders were soaked again as water ran off his hat against the lamp light, but he didn't care. Lee-one was waving now, making exaggerated motions with his arm. Lee-two returned the wave, and her father turned and headed back up the slope. Even with the sound of the flood-waters, Jake could hear that he was singing. The words were foreign to him but the tune was familiar. He was singing the hymn, "On Our Way Rejoicing", and at the top of the hill, he set the lantern down and turned to wave again. Once again Lee-two waved back, and she stood watching until her father's shadowy figure had disappeared over the hill and the glow from the lantern was lost in the darkness. She turned back to Jake, and her face was shining.

"You are getting wet again, Mr. Sullivan," she said.

Jake nodded, "I reckon."

Handing him the lantern she said, "Thank you for your coat. We should go back inside where it is warm and dry."

As they headed up the slope, Lee-two slipped and Jake reached quickly to take her arm. She turned, smiled her thanks and said, "Either this dress of mine is no good for walking or I am out of practice."

Jake followed Lee-two into the cabin, but stopped just inside the door. "I think I'll just grab my bedroll and head for the barn loft," he said. "It's been a full day."

Lee-two turned to face him. "Are you sure?" she asked. "I think I should be the one to sleep out there. After all, this is your place. I do not feel right about it."

Jake shook his head. "I may be a horse thief," he said. "But I draw the line at makin' a lady sleep out in the barn."

Lee-two smiled. "It feels good to get to be a lady for a day. It feels good not to be afraid. It is very tiring work being afraid."

"That's an interesting way to put it." Jake said thoughtfully. "I think you're right though." He crossed the room to his bunk and began rolling up his blankets. "Your pa's got a long walk home. I feel bad we couldn't help him."

As he turned for the door Lee-two said, "The walk home will be easy now that his heart is light."

Jake turned, stood and regarded her a moment. "I suppose it will," he said. "I suppose it will."

He crossed the room to the door, and as his hand found the latch Lee-two said, "Mr. Sullivan?"

He turned to face her.

"I do not think this full day will be complete until I tell you my story."

Jake paused, and then nodded, "Alright," he said. "Don't feel like you have to though. I doubt my story was a fair trade."

"What do you mean?" Lee-two asked.

Jake thought a moment then said, "My story didn't involve anyone else, and I had nothing to be afraid of."

"That is why I would like to tell you, Mr. Sullivan," Lee-two said earnestly. "I do not want to be afraid anymore. I realize that when someone else knows my secret, it is easier to carry. I would like you to know the rest. It will not take long, I promise."

Jake shook his head. "I ain't worried about that. Truth is I'd like to know. I just want you to know you're entitled to your secrets if you want to keep them that way."

Lee-two smiled and said, "Maybe we should sit down. It could take more time than what I said."

Jake set his bedroll by the door and followed Lee-two to the table. When they'd taken their seats, she began speaking.

"My father became a convert to Christianity shortly after the death of my mother. It had been her faith for a long time, and a missionary came to our home and prayed for her every day when she was too weak to get out of bed. I do not remember this because I was too young. I only know because father told me."

Jake nodded and waited.

"It was Mr. Tanner's kindness to my mother and our family that touched my father's heart, and after she died, his kindness and concern for our well-being continued. Mr. Tanner and my father became like brothers, and not long after, father went to work for him, tending his garden, minding the house and cooking the meals. I was raised in Mr. Tanner's house and went to school with the missionary children. Father was so proud that I was receiving a good education. These were very happy times for us, though at first my father missed my mother terribly.

When I was fourteen years old, Mr. Tanner became sick, and it was decided it would be best for him to travel back to America for treatment. He became very weak, and my father thought we should accompany him on his journey as he was in need of care. Mr. Tanner was grateful for the company, and was convinced he would be back to China soon.

He died on the ship, however, and was buried at sea. When we arrived in Astoria there was no one to meet us and we had almost no money. Father decided to look for work in order to pay our fare back to China, but he soon found that many Americans did not like the Chinese and so work was not easy to find. There was a small Chinese community in the city, and father learned that they were hiring Chinese workers to help build the railway. Father thought he would only be gone a short time, but he did not want to leave me in Astoria. He had heard some terrible stories about what had happened to some Chinese women, and so it was decided I would pretend to be a boy. We traveled by boat a long way east up a big river, and soon we were living in a tent camp that was always moving further east, always moving further from the sea and a boat to take us home. Father worked long hours and I got a job as a camp cook. These were hard times, especially in the winter and many men were killed in accidents. There was much tension between the Chinese and American workers too, and many were afraid. I did not see my father much, only late at night and early in the morning. He was saving money though, and he would always say to me, "Soon my little bird, soon you will be flying home". One day there was a big explosion in a tunnel and many men were killed. My father was injured badly and lost the use of his arm. He could no longer go to work, and he was very discouraged. Then came the terrible night…"

Lee-two paused and looked down at her hands, her brow furrowed as if it hurt her to remember. Jake didn't say anything and presently she continued.

"Father was lying injured on his cot, and four Chinese men came bursting into our tent. They had realized father was not spending much money, and they knew he must have some hidden somewhere. A man held a knife to my throat and threatened to kill me if father didn't show him where it was. They took it all, and when they left father broke down and wept. He kept saying over and over again that God had abandoned us. I was trying to comfort him when suddenly outside we heard screaming and shooting. When we looked out of the tent we saw flames reaching high in the sky and people running madly in all directions. My father grabbed my hand and we fled into the night. He told me later that a white man had been murdered, and that they had blamed it on the Chinese. There had been much talk that the Americans would retaliate, but he had kept it from me as he did not want me to be afraid. We climbed a hill to the east, and when we looked back it seemed our whole camp was on fire.

The next day we managed to hide in some empty wagons that had brought railway ties to the camps, and these took us even further east. We came to a small town at the edge of some mountains, and father got a job sweeping and cleaning at a gambling house as we were hungry and he needed to buy food. He only worked there one morning, because a young man who had fallen asleep drunk on the front step the night before asked him what he was doing trying to sweep with only one arm. Father replied that he had to do something. This young man asked father if he could cook, and when father said yes, the young man offered him a job. It was Nathan Daniels, and I have no idea what he was doing so far from home, but he paid for our stage fare and brought us here. That was almost three years ago, and father is still saving money to get us back to China."

VII

Though he was exhausted, Jake lay awake well into the night, his mind wandering randomly from one of the day's many happenings to another. He fell asleep to the sound of rain on the barn roof and woke to the steady roar of the river. He lay still for a while, yesterday's events coming again to mind, then he crawled from his bedroll, put on his boots and hat and climbed down the ladder from the loft. Stepping out the barn door, he glanced toward the cabin and saw smoke climbing from the chimney. Pausing a moment, he stood and took in the morning. The rain had washed the tired air, and it smelled new and alive. Birds were singing in the day, and though heavy clouds shrouded the peaks, overhead the sky was clean and blue. Wispy fingers of mist clung to the low ground and the wet grass was silver in the early light.

Before heading for the cabin, Jake made his way down to the overturned wagon. The river had risen during the night and one rear wheel was completely submerged. Pulling aside the tarp, he took a look at what he had in the way of groceries. Stooping, he re-packed several cans into a wooden crate, then turned and lugged them up to the cabin. Again the door swung open before he could knock, and Lee-two stepped aside to let him enter.

"Good morning, Mr. Sullivan. Did you sleep well?"

Jake nodded, noting that although Lee-two was wearing her own shirt, she was still using the wool blanket for a make-shift dress. She'd found a short piece of rope somewhere and had it tied snuggly around her slender waist.

"Yes, ma'am," he replied, "How about you?"

"I slept very well, but I was the one who had the bed. Breakfast is almost ready."

Jake glanced over at the stove and saw a stack of flap-jacks in the warming oven. "It sure smells good in here, Lee-two," he said. "I think you're spoilin' me." He set the wooden crate by the door, and as he straightened up continued speaking. "I'll just keep fetchin' things in from the wagon, so just give me a yell when it's time to sit up."

After breakfast, Jake tried to help with the cleanup, but Lee-two insisted she was fine, so he headed outside to catch Big Jake. The team was standing together at the far end of the horse pasture, and though Jake didn't go to investigate, the lame horse was bearing weight on all four feet. He slipped a halter on his gelding, and the blaze-faced bay followed them down the alley. Jake shut him in a small pen by himself, and after he'd saddled up, rode out to bring in the remuda. As the horses filed in through the gate ahead of him, he saw the cabin door open and Lee-two come strolling over. She tried to climb the rail fence, but the blanket she wore made it difficult, so she turned and found the gate. She stopped and watched from a distance as Jake cut a short coupled black filly into the breaking pen, and when he'd swung the gate shut, she called over.

"Do you mind if I watch?" she asked.

"Not at all," Jake replied. "You can come over closer if you'd like. Just stay outside the pen."

With Lee-two standing quietly watching, Jake spent a pleasant morning putting the first ride on a couple of horses. After the rain, the sun was no longer heavy and oppressive, but felt warm and pleasant on his face and shoulders. As he was stripping his saddle off a sorrel colt, Lee-two walked around the outside of the corral toward him.

Looking through the rails she said, "It looks like a dance."

Jake turned toward her. "What's that?" he asked.

"It looks like a dance," she said again, "you in the middle and the horse moving around you. It is like you are speaking without making any sound. I think it is beautiful."

Jake smiled. "What about that last little bit," he said. "That fella had a little buck in him."

"I don't think he was trying very hard," Lee-two said. "I think that was part of the dance also."

Jake smiled and shook his head. "Funny thing," he said. "I ate the biggest breakfast I've had in a while, and I'm already feelin' hungry."

"I can go make something," Lee-two offered.

"That's alright. I can't stop thinkin' about those left over flap jacks." Jake followed Lee-two through the gate, and then walked beside her to the cabin.

"Do you give the horses names?" she asked suddenly.

Jake shook his head. "Not usually," he said. "Sometimes I do, but most of the time they ain't around long enough."

Lee-two stopped at the door and turned to face him. "That black horse you rode first is very beautiful. I think it should have a name."

"Maybe you should name her," Jake suggested.

Lee-two paused, and then nodding, looked up at Jake and said, "I will think about it." Looking around she continued, "It is very nice outside. I think we should eat out here."

"The ground might be a bit wet for sittin' on," Jake said. "I suppose I could spread my slicker out on the ground though."

"I would like that." Lee-two said. "I will get the food and the coffee."

Jake spread his slicker on the sunny side of the cabin, and they sat down with their backs to the wall. As he ate Jake remembered Lee-two's comment about naming the horses.

"What about you?" he said, turning to face her. "What about your name? I doubt your pa calls you Lee-two."

Lee-two smiled and shook her head, "No, he calls me by my Chinese name."

"What is it? I feel kinda bad I never thought to ask you before this."

Lee-two shrugged her shoulders. "I do not mind. My name would be hard for you to say."

"Try me," Jake said.

Lee-two smiled and said, "Shee'ou nee ow."

Jake raised his eyebrows. "Can you spell it with English letters?" he asked.

Lee-two laughed. "Yes, but that will only make it worse."

"Come on, spell it," Jake insisted.

"X-i-a-o, n-i-a-o."

Jake turned and looked away, then smiling, looked back and said, "You're right. I might have to stick to Lee-two."

Lee-two smiled, "I do not mind," she said. "I have gotten quite used to it. It is not what you call someone, but how you feel in your heart about them that matters. I know you do not think less of me and my father because we are Chinese. I knew this ever since you helped me unload the wagon."

Jake looked away and was silent for a moment. Then he said, "What does it mean?" Then he added clumsily, "Sheeoo – Ne-ew."

Lee-two smiled again. "That was not too bad. Maybe you would make a good Chinese after all. It means, Small Bird."

"Small Bird," Jake echoed. "A little chickadee."

They ate the rest of their meal in comfortable silence. When Jake had taken his last swallow of coffee, he said, "I think I'll try ridin' the man-killer this afternoon."

Lee-two turned quickly and said, "Do you think that is wise?"

Jake thought for a moment before answering. "I could be wrong, I guess," he said finally. "I wasn't here to see what went on the first time around, but that horse don't strike me as bein' mean. I figure we already got us a bit of an understandin' and anyway, if I am wrong he's gonna have to prove it to me."

"You be careful, Mr. Sullivan. I saw the other man when they brought him in. I am surprised he has not died."

Jake looked at Lee-two seriously. "I'll be careful. If that horse is dangerous I'll get him to tell me before I go too far."

"You will get him to tell you?" Lee-two asked.

Jake nodded. "Horses can tell you a lot of things if you take the time to notice."

—⟋⟋⟍—

Jake mounted his gelding and rode up the alley to the pen where the blaze-faced bay waited. Without dismounting, and paying no particular attention to the colt, he swung the gate wide, then turned and headed for the breaking pen. He was just riding through the gate when he heard the bay's hoof beats coming up behind him. The horse trotted on past, then stopped at the far side of the corral and turned to watch him. Jake studied him a moment before closing the gate, admiring the horse's strong hip and sloping shoulder. The gelding displayed none of the fear that had ruled him the first time Jake had worked him, but seemed more curious than anything. Jake decided a little review wouldn't hurt, however, so he began to move him around the outside of the pen from the back of Big Jake. At first the colt shook his head in mild protest, but he was soon moving in a relaxed trot. Jake kept it up for a few minutes, alternating between circling left to right, then right to left. He watched the horse closely, and when the bay began to open and close his mouth in a sign of submission, Jake reined in and waited at the center of the corral. The colt hesitated only a moment, then came over to stand with his head against Jake's leg, and Jake reached out to scratch him behind the ears.

"That's a good fella," he said. "That's what we like to see." He moved his hand down onto the horse's neck, then backed Big Jake up a couple of steps and scratched the colt on the withers. After a few minutes he turned and rode to the gate and the blaze-faced bay fell in behind.

Jake dismounted and led his gelding out of the corral, shutting the bay colt inside. He threw his reins over a rail, stripped off his saddle, and carried it back into the breaking pen. When he entered on foot, the bay's head came up sharply, and the horse snorted, then trotted off to watch from the opposite side of the pen. Jake dropped his saddle, and after taking off his rope, pushed it half under the gate. He glanced quickly to where a heavy leather halter hung from a post, and then turned his attention to the bay. The colt eyed him warily as he slowly built a loop and turned to walk to the center of the corral. Jake stopped, and the horse bobbed his head nervously, his nostrils flaring, then bolted hard around the outside of the pen before coming to a sliding stop at the gate where Jake's gelding waited unconcerned on the other side.

As of yet Jake had put no pressure on the bay, but stood calmly at the center of the corral while the colt see-sawed frantically back and forth in front of the gate, his body a tight-coiled spring of raw power and rippling muscles. His hindquarters grew wide as he spun on his hocks to pound in short powerful strides around the outside of the pen, making three laps before coming to a nervous stop at the gate again. He turned wide-eyed to Jake, and then wheeled away, his face and chest against the rails, and then he was running. This time he made several laps before coming to a stop at the gate, his sides heaving up and down while sweat dripped from glistening flanks. Jake let him stand for a while, and then took a slight step toward the gelding's hip, giving one slow swing with his loop. The horse was off again, and now Jake kept him moving, around and around, his hooves sounding an even rhythm and his head slowly coming down. Jake shifted his position ever so slightly, putting pressure on the colt's shoulder, and the horse turned to run hard in the opposite direction before slowing to an even steady stride.

Jake kept him moving that way for several laps, then turned him back the other way again. The colt was watching him now and only made it halfway around the pen before he was licking his lips while opening and closing his mouth. Jake stopped, standing still and quiet while the bay came to a shuffling stop. The horse turned his face toward him, his breathing hard and heavy, and Jake waited. Several loaded seconds passed before the colt turned and walked to stand head down and quiet beside the man. Jake reached out and put a gentle hand on the gelding's face; the horse didn't pull away, but seemed relieved that it was over. Then Jake was scratching him along the jaw and up by the ears, speaking in low reassuring tones that offered comfort. He kept this up for a few minutes, and when he turned to walk away the horse followed, his face inches from his back.

Jake wandered randomly around the pen, and wherever he went the colt went too. Several times Jake stopped to reassure the horse with quiet words and gentle hands on his face and neck before turning to walk some more. Eventually he walked over to where the halter hung from a post, took it down and slipped it on the bay who took it without a fight. The horse then followed him over to where his saddle lay beneath the rail gate, and with the halter shank hanging loose, Jake unceremoniously picked it up and threw it on the colt's back. The horse stood calmly while he cinched up, and then, after a reassuring pat on the neck, Jake took hold of the shank, put a foot in the stirrup, and swung into the saddle. The colt didn't move, but took the weight standing calm and still while Jake scratched his neck and quietly praised him. After several minutes Jake swung down, and making a gentle clucking sound before moving out, led the bay around the corral. He mounted up again, and again the horse stood still. Jake rocked gently back and forth in the saddle, then with movements slow and unhurried, he swung down, made the same clucking noise and moved the colt out again, making one full lap around the corral.

"Whoa big fella." Jake said softly, coming to a stop himself.

The bay colt stopped and Jake rewarded him with a scratch on the forehead. After standing quietly for a while, Jake clucked and moved out again. He repeated this several times, and then mounted up. After a short pause, he bumped the colt lightly with his calves while making the same clucking sound. The bay took a couple of tentative steps forward then stopped. Jake offered more words of gentle praise, and then sat patient and still. The sun was warm on his face, and the sound of the river was a pleasant thing, and then Jake coaxed the horse into motion again. This time the gelding took several steps before coming to a stop, and again he was rewarded with gentle words and time to think things over. Soon Jake had the colt moving around the outside of the pen in a willing and easy trot, and it seemed to him that all was well with the world.

Cliff Barry set his empty coffee cup down on the table with enough force to betray his frustration, then looked at the man seated across from him and said, "I wish it was better news Abe, but that's just the way she lays."

Abe Daniels shook his head in disbelief. "Over three hundred short! How can that be? We must be gettin' rustled?"

Barry shook his head. "I don't think so. We've been ridin' pretty hard now for awhile an' no one's seen any sign that points that way. Arnie's crew's havin' a pretty good gather up north an' likely woulda done better if they hadn't been short-handed."

"Short-handed?"

Barry leaned back in his chair and crossed his big arms on his chest, hesitating as if he were reluctant to speak.

"It's my boy, ain't it," Abe said, his voice showing tired resignation.

Barry nodded. "Arnie sent him to comb the breaks to the northeast, but he never made it further than Carmody's I reckon. Arnie's got a couple of boys ridin' that country now so I figure a few more head should turn up."

For a while no one spoke, and then Barry got to his feet. Abe looked up at him and asked, "How about them white-face critters; are they in pretty good shape?"

Again Barry hesitated, and then said reluctantly, "The ones we're findin' are in good shape. We ain't found too many of them to be honest."

"What?!" Abe bellowed. "What do you mean you ain't found too many of them?"

Barry shrugged his shoulders. "We've found a few scattered here and there, but right now they're makin' up a big part of the short count. We're missin' mosta the young stuff too."

Abe's eyes grew bright and hot. "Then I'd say we got a rustlin' problem! Why wasn't I told sooner?"

"I kept thinkin' they'd turn up," Barry said. "I still think they will in time and I'm pretty sure it ain't rustlers. The way I see it, when them big outfits to the south finish their fall gathers your count will look a sight better."

"I can't wait that long and you know it!" Abe growled. "My note's due at the bank by month's end and I'm cash poor right now. It took all I had to bring them Herefords in here, and I need to sell off them steers to make the payment!"

"Well let's hope Arnie's crew turns 'em up when they finish ridin' the breaks." Barry watched Abe, who didn't respond but sat staring off at nothing. He could tell the man was worried, and he put a hand on the door to leave before turning quickly back. "Oh, I almost forgot. Carmody says your boy's piled up quite a debt at the faro table. Figures he might be gettin' in over his head."

Abe looked up with eyes that smoldered and snapped, "Tell him not to give him any credit!"

"I ain't tellin' a man how to run his business," Barry said, "and Nathan's full growed."

Abe glared at him, and then Barry turned and stepped outside, closing the door behind him. He paused a moment on the front porch, feeling a twinge of guilt for the lies he'd told the man who had trusted him all these years. Not being given to reflection, however, he was able to quickly shrug it off, and stepping down the stairs, strode purposefully across the compound. He was halfway to the barn when he heard the footfalls of a horse behind him. Turning he saw Chance Adler, one of Cob's crew approaching on a hammer-headed paint. Glancing nervously over his shoulder, he put his hands on his hips and waited for Adler to rein in in front of him.

"I thought I left you with the cows up on the mesa," Barry said accusingly.

"Palliser's with 'em," the skinny rider replied. He turned and spat a stream of tobacco juice onto the ground, and when he looked back to Barry he had dark dribble running into his sparse blonde beard, which he didn't bother to wipe away.

"How's the grass holdin up?" Barry asked.

"It's gettin' chewed down, but this rain'll help."

"Anyway," Barry said, his voice condescending, "you ain't supposed to show your face around here."

Adler looked back at him, his eyes bored. Then without a word, he turned his horse and proceeded to ride out the way he'd come.

"Wait a minute!" Barry barked.

Adler stopped his horse but didn't bother to turn around.

"I guess you wouldn't ride down here for nothin'," Barry conceded. "What's on your mind?"

Adler reined back around. "That new bronc stomper you hired…"

"Yeah, what about him?"

"He knows about the cattle up on the mesa."

Barry's eyes were instantly hard and bright. "You sure?" he asked.

Adler nodded. "He cut the sign o' that last bunch the boys brought in same day you was up there."

Barry's eyes darted up toward the big house while he chewed on his bottom lip. Looking back to Adler he asked again, "You're sure?"

"You already asked me that," was Adler's response.

Barry was silent for a few moments, then he said with quiet conviction, "We're gonna have to do somethin' about that."

"I figured so," Adler said. A subtle eagerness crept into his voice as he continued, "Want me to kill 'im?"

Barry didn't answer immediately, but rubbed his chin, deep in thought. "No," he said. "Not right now anyway. I got a better idea."

Adler looked at him, an unspoken question on his brow. Barry continued speaking, his voice dark and quiet.

"The man's a horse thief," he said. "He stole horses once so he can do it again."

VIII

It was three days before the flood waters subsided enough that Jake felt it would be safe to cross the river. A sky that had forgotten how to rain now seemed to carry moisture in every cloud, and each day was a mix of reluctant sunshine and scattered showers. The thirsty land was drinking it up, and though it was late August, it was giving back a fresh carpet of green.

Jake had tried putting the wagon back on its wheels with a rope over a back hub, but though his gelding gave a mighty effort, he was unable to get enough traction in the wet ground. The injured draft horse was still a bit off, so Lee-two would have been unable to take the wagon home anyway.

Jake led his big gelding and the black filly to the barn, tied them to the hitch rail, and then headed to the cabin for breakfast. Because of Lee-two's interest in the filly, he'd been keeping the horse in the small pasture and putting extra time on both her and the blood bay colt. Both were showing themselves to be willing horses with a lot of try, and their progress gave Jake a deep satisfaction.

At the cabin door he knocked lightly then stepped inside. Lee-two was at the stove, and she turned and smiled as he hung his hat by the door. She was wearing her trousers again in anticipation of the trip back to the home ranch.

"Breakfast is not ready, but I filled your coffee cup," she said.

Jake nodded and smiled his thanks, then took a seat at the table. He watched as Lee-two added wood to the stove, and when she turned their eyes met. She smiled tentatively and looked quickly away, vigorously stirring the pancake batter.

Jake continued to watch her, then cleared his throat and said, "You're gonna need to do somethin' about that coat you lost."

Lee-two looked up and Jake shifted uncomfortably in his chair before he continued.

"I don't quite know how to say it proper, but it's pretty obvious you ain't a boy."

Lee-two looked quickly down at the stove. "I am glad of that," she said quietly, "but I have been thinking about this problem also."

"Have you got another coat at home?" Jake asked.

Lee-two shook her head. "No. I will have to wear one of my father's until I can get something else."

Jake took a sip of his coffee. "How about I cut a hole in the middle of that blanket you've been wearin'," he said. "You can slip your head through and use it for a poncho."

"A poncho? What is a poncho?"

Jake smiled. "I reckon it's a blanket with a hole for your head, kind of a poor man's coat."

Lee-two hesitated. "I will need to do something," she said. "I hate to ruin your blanket though."

"It's a company blanket I reckon. I figure they probably owe you a new coat anyway."

When Lee-two brought the food to the table they ate in silence, and Jake was feeling oddly melancholy. He knew it was because Lee-two's time at the Two Canyons cabin was over, and his feelings surprised him. He looked across the table at her, and wondered if she wasn't feeling the same way. She was less talkative than usual, and even seemed a little awkward. Jake put down his fork, feeling a little awkward himself. "You lookin' forward to seein' your pa?" he asked.

Lee-two nodded. "He will be anxious to see me, and I know he needs my help, but I am not looking forward to being a boy again."

"Do you think you have to?" Jake asked. "If you showed up wearin' a dress you'd sure take the wind out of their sails. Those boys would be fallin' all over themselves tryin' to get in your good books."

Lee-two smiled, but it was a sad smile. "You are a kind man, Mr. Sullivan," she said. "I am afraid everyone is not like you, especially when it comes to a Chinese girl. This is one reason why father wants to get me back to China. He says…"

Lee-two didn't finish her thought, but Jake knew where she was going with it, and he didn't want to finish it for her, so he changed the subject.

"I'll put my saddle on Big Jake, so you can ride him. I hope you're okay ridin' without stirrups, 'cause I don't think I can get them short enough."

"Which horse are you going to ride? Will you not need your saddle?"

"I'm fine ridin' bareback," Jake said. "I woulda rode Barry's gelding, but I kicked him out with the young stuff 'cause he's got an abscess and won't be usable for quite some time. I'm gonna ride that pretty black filly you're so fond of. Did you ever think of a name for her?"

Lee-two shook her head. "Not one that is good enough," she said.

The food was gone and his coffee cup was empty, but Jake felt a reluctance to leave. He wanted to tell Lee-two that he'd enjoyed her company, but didn't quite know how to go about it. He got to his feet, turned to her and said, "Thanks again for breakfast, Lee-two. I ain't lookin' forward to havin' to choke down my own cookin' again."

"You are most welcome, Mr. Sullivan, but it was much easier only having to cook for two."

"That may be so," Jake said, "but I reckon with the crew gone I probably spoiled your vacation."

Lee-two looked as if she were about to say something but then changed her mind.

Jake waited for an awkward moment, and then said, "I reckon I'll go saddle up."

Lee-two nodded. "It will not take me long to wash up these dishes," she said. "The water is already hot."

Stepping outside, Jake glanced at the sky, hoping the rain would hold off as he only had one slicker. He then picked his way around the puddles to the barn. Once Big Jake was saddled, he looked through the extra bridles hanging on the wall and found one to use on the filly. He was slipping it on her head when he heard the cabin door come open.

"I'll bring the horses over, Lee-two," he called. "No use you gettin' your shoes muddy." He led the horses up to the cabin, and Lee-two looked at him apprehensively.

"I have not ridden a horse very often," she said.

"Don't worry about it. Jake'll take good care of you. Just trust him. Here let me give you a leg up."

After helping Lee-two into the saddle, Jake swung up onto the black filly. The horse side-stepped nervously, not used to the feel of a rider without a saddle, but Jake sat quiet and let her work it out. His relaxed attitude won her over, and when she was standing calmly he moved her down toward the river. At the bank she balked and snorted, and though the river was nothing like the day of the flood, it still ran deep and fast. Jake looked over his shoulder at Lee-two and said, "I think you'll have to cross first. This little girl's a bit timid but I think she'll follow Jake all right."

Lee-two looked at the water, and Jake saw fear in her eyes.

"You'll be fine, Lee-two," he said. "You can trust Big Jake, I promise."

Lee-two nodded uncertainly. "I am not sure which Jake you are talking about," she said.

Jake looked at her seriously. "I'll do my best too," he said. He glanced at the river then looked back to Lee-two. "Would you like me to ride him across and back first?" he asked.

Lee-two shook her head seriously. "No. I will be fine. I trust both Big Jakes."

She rode past him, and the big gelding struck boldly out into the current. Jake was quick to turn the filly's nose in right behind. She hesitated only momentarily and then followed the gray into the fast moving river. They splashed across as the water rushed beneath them, and Jake saw that it was up past the gelding's hocks. Soon they were scrambling out the other side, and when Jake pulled up beside Lee-two, he saw her knuckles were white as she gripped the saddle horn. Smiling at her, he said, "I think I just thought of a name for this little filly."

"Mr. Sullivan!" Lee-two said shaking her head in exasperation. "How could you have been thinking of anything except getting across alive?"

Jake laughed. "That's why I sent you first. I wanted to make sure it was safe."

Lee-two looked at him seriously. "I was very scared," she said. Then after a brief pause she asked, "So what is this name?"

Jake didn't answer right away. Then he looked at her and said, "Chickadee. I think I'll call this pretty little horse Chickadee."

Lee-two looked away and didn't say anything. Then as they turned to ride up the slope away from the river she looked appreciatively at Jake and said, "I am riding a horse that is named after you, and you are riding one that is named after me."

—〰—

Though the sky was threatening, they made the home ranch without getting rained on. The yard was empty, but there was smoke coming from the cook house chimney. Jake dismounted out front, and was about to help Lee-two from the saddle when he heard the sound of hooves on the mud road. Turning he saw four riders coming through the front gate.

"I guess I am a Chinese boy who cannot speak English again."

Jake turned to face Lee-two as the riders approached.

"Thank you for everything, Mr. Sullivan," she said softly, and then the sound of a trotting horse was upon them. Jake turned back to see the ugly face of Cliff Barry, who seemed surprised to see him. He was a couple of horse lengths in front of the other men, and he was riding the bald faced chestnut.

"I see our chink boy finally made it back," he said as he drew rein. "How come he never brought the wagon?"

Lee-two was dismounting awkwardly, and when her feet hit the ground, she glanced from Jake to Barry, then with eyes lowered in submission, quickly climbed the steps and entered the cookhouse. Jake could hear her father's excited exclamation, and then the door swung shut. Barry was watching, waiting for an answer.

"The wagon tipped over when he was crossing the flooded river. I couldn't get it back on its wheels, and one of the team's lamed up a bit."

The other riders were dismounting now, and Barry turned to face them. "Go on in, Arnie," he said. "I'll join you in a minute." Looking back to Jake he asked, "The wagon tipped over?"

Jake nodded. "The water was too deep and it went over when the current hit the box. The team got it drug almost clear of the water before they went down."

Barry's look betrayed mild disbelief. "Lucky little chink," he said. "I'm surprised he didn't drown. Anyway, how are you makin' out up there? You got most of them horses topped off?"

"I'm a bit better than halfway through."

"I suppose the creek's washed out the trail at the top end of the north canyon."

"I wouldn't know. I ain't been back up there."

Barry paused and seemed about to say something else. He hesitated, then glanced at the sky and said, "Well I guess you'd best make tracks if you want to beat the rain."

Jake watched Barry's back as he mounted the steps to enter the cookhouse. He was surprised that he'd made no mention of when he wanted horses brought down. He was surprised too that he hadn't been told to leave the black filly behind. This was a relief because he wanted the chance to put more rides on her. As far as he was concerned she was Lee-two's horse, though he knew when it came right down to it he had no say in the matter. He tightened the cinch on Big Jake, glanced at the cook-shack, hesitated, then stepped up onto the veranda and opened the door. Barry looked up from the table as he entered.

"I'm just grabbin' a coffee," Jake said, then stepped through the door into the kitchen. Lee-one was at the table pouring flour into a mixing bowl, and Jake acknowledged him with a quick nod. Lee-two turned from the stove as he entered, and he saw a light come into her eyes. He quickly crossed the room to her, took the coffee pot from the stove, and when he turned to face her she was looking up at him. Jake stood awkwardly for a moment, and then said quietly, "I just wanted to say goodbye."

Lee-two nodded, but didn't say anything. Lee-one had stopped in his work and stood watching them. Jake glanced at him, and then looked back to Lee-two who hadn't moved.

"I'd like to come for a visit sometime," he said.

The corner of Lee-two's mouth trembled ever so slightly and she said softly, "I would like that."

Jake glanced back to Lee-one who was still watching, then moved to take a cup down from the counter. When he'd poured his coffee, he went back to the stove and returned the coffee pot. He turned again to face Lee-two, who was standing close, and not knowing what else to do, he extended his hand. She took it and they shook hands formally.

"I'll be seein' you," Jake said.

"Good," was all Lee-two said in reply.

Jake let go of her hand, nodded again to Lee-one, then turned and left the kitchen. He took a seat by himself away from the other men, and when he'd gulped down his coffee, got up and left.

—⁂—

Jake was about halfway back to the Two Canyons when the air cooled off and a slow steady drizzle began to fall. He shrugged into his slicker and sucked his hands as far as he could up into his sleeves in an attempt to keep his fingers warm. He reached the last bend in the trail, and was surprised when he smelled wood smoke. Cresting the bank above the river, he looked across to see four saddled horses standing heads down and hip shot in front of the cabin. Blue gray smoke rose briefly from the chimney, then hit an invisible ceiling and leveled off before blending into the dull haze of rain. Jake waited under the dripping boughs of an evergreen, feeling a curious reluctance to go forward. He summed it up to not wanting to share the cabin with strangers, who he guessed were from one of the round up crews and were looking for re-mounts. Nothing could be done about it, however, so he put his horse in motion and slid down the greasy bank, noting that the river was on the rise again.

As he pulled up to the cabin he reasoned that had the four riders been planning to spend the night, they would have off saddled. In anticipation of helping gather and sort the colts, he turned Chickadee loose with the team and the bay before dismounting at the barn. Shoulders hunched against a raw wind coming off the slopes, he trudged through the mud to the cabin. Pushing the door open, he stepped inside, greeted by welcome warm air and cold indifferent faces. Jake noted absently that there was mud tracked across the floor as one of the riders rose to meet him. He was a tall, skinny man with unkempt blonde hair and an angular hawk-like face. He stopped and stood feet apart in front of Jake.

"We movin' some horses?" Jake asked.

"You might say that." The tall rider responded. He hooked his thumbs in his belt and stood regarding Jake, an odd light in his pale green eyes. "You gonna take off that slicker?" he asked.

Jake thought the question a strange one and none of the other riders had made a move to rise. "Only if we're not goin' right away. I could do with a coffee I guess," he responded.

"You may as well lose the slicker," was the blonde rider's reply.

Jake paused, meeting the other man's gaze. Something wasn't right here, but he had no idea why or what. "Alright," he said.

While the other man watched, he took off his oilskin, and as he turned to hang it by the door, he heard the distinct sharp click of a pistol being cocked. Turning slowly back he found himself looking into the barrel of a gun, and behind it, sneering eyes on a crooked face.

"Now why a man would see fit to travel around with no gun is beyond me," the skinny rider said.

"What's goin' on?" Jake asked quietly.

"Why, you're about to live up to your reputation, horse thief."

Jake's head came up in surprise, and his look betrayed an unspoken question.

"You're about to steal some horses, and me an' the boys are gonna follow you and catch you red-handed. Where it goes from there you can probably figure out for yourself."

Jake stood stock still, his mind racing. He remembered Barry's surprise at seeing him at the ranch, and his suggestion that he hit the trail quick to beat the rain. Barry had come up with a convenient plan to get him out of the way, but just how "out of the way", Jake wasn't sure. He was also unsure why Barry thought it was necessary, but his instincts told him it had something to do with the cattle sign up on the mesa.

The other riders were getting to their feet and the skinny gunman said, "You may as well put your slicker back on now that I know you ain't heeled."

Jake looked at him but didn't move.

"Now!" the man snarled.

The pistol came up to eye level, and Jake hesitated only a moment then turned and obediently took his slicker from the wall. When he'd put it on, he stepped out into the rain and the others followed.

"Taylor, you an' Orrin go gather up a jag o' them ponies," the blonde rider said. "It don't much matter which ones I reckon. Just so as we leave a good set o' tracks in case Sheriff Kingman don't take Barry's word for it."

Without a word, two of the men mounted their horses and rode for the top pasture. The fourth man, an older hand with a heavy moustache, stepped into the saddle, then palmed his pistol and covered Jake while the blonde rider mounted up.

"Okay horse thief. It's your turn."

Under the cover of two guns, Jake walked the short dis-tance to the barn and then swung up on Big Jake. The pasture gate had been left open, and they rode through it, then off to the south to wait for the herd to come by.

"Well look there!" the blonde rider exclaimed. "That's the same bronc that busted up Howard!"

Just across the rail fence, and less than twenty yards away, the blaze-faced bay was standing head up and broadside, watching the two riders bringing in the horses. No sooner had the blonde gunman spoken, than he took his pistol off Jake to line it up on the horse. Quick as thought, and oblivious of the gun that covered him, Jake leapt from the saddle. His left hand grabbed the gunman's collar while he reached around with his right to try and slap the pistol off line. Jake heard the gun go off, and then the skinny rider's horse reared high, sending both men tumbling to the soggy ground. Jake landed heavily on top of the blonde rider, and still gripping his coat, grabbed a fistful of hair with his free hand and began slamming the man's face violently into the mud. Lights burst in his brain and then he knew nothing.

IX

Jake became gradually aware of a faint humming sound, pulsing like a heartbeat growing steadily louder, and then the pain brought him back to consciousness. At first it was the pain in his head, throbbing with the same rhythm as the ringing in his ears, and then it was a sharp stabbing in his side that came and went with every breath he took. Jake opened his eyes and it was a while before they would focus. He was staring stupidly at his hands, which were swollen and tied with a rawhide cord to his saddle horn. A big drop of red water fell on them, spread out and disappeared, only to be replaced by another. He realized slowly that he was bare headed, and that the rain was washing blood from a wound on his scalp. Little by little his mind cleared; little by little he remembered.

"You got a hard head."

Jake slowly turned his face to the speaker. It was the man with the moustache.

"I had to hit you twice before I could pull you off him. Adler woulda shot you where you laid if I hadn't stopped him. He sure put the boots to you though."

Jake turned his face away and let his head hang, swinging back and forth with his horse's gait. He was having a hard time framing his thoughts, as it seemed to take too much effort to concentrate.

"We didn't kill the horse."

Jake turned again to face the speaker.

"We didn't kill the horse. I thought maybe you'd want to know. I figured if a man would risk his life for him he must be some kinda horse. He's sure a looker anyway."

After that they rode in silence. Jake slowly became aware of his surroundings, and he realized the man who rode beside him held the reins to his gelding. They were following a narrow trail that clung to the shoulder of a steep side hill. The downhill slope was heavily timbered, and far below Jake caught the occasional glimpse of a mad tumbling stream. Above them the trees thinned out, and a slope of loose scree ended abruptly at the base of a tall gray cliff that lost itself in drifting clouds. They were several horse lengths behind the other riders, who were trailing a loose herd of horses.

"Can you hear me?"

Jake turned and looked at the man beside him.

"Good. Pretend you can't."

Jake let his head sag again and waited.

"Adler's gonna kill you when we get to the meadows over the ridge. I don't think highly of the idea myself. I figure a horse thief on the run serves our purpose every bit as good as a dead one. The story runs somethin' like this. We came to get some horses and found you'd run off with most of 'em. We trailed you over this here ridge, found your camp at the meadows and shot it out with you. The country's got one less horse thief, and we saved the Anchor D horses, so who's gonna kick?"

The man with the moustache fell silent, and Jake waited, wondering what was next. A short time later the man spoke again.

"Half a mile further up there's a slide on the downhill side runs almost to the river. She's mighty steep but I think you can make it. I'll cut your wrists loose just before we get there, then you can slug me and make your break. I'll be shootin, but I'll take care to shoot high and wide. I'm the only one here with a rifle, so if you can get out of pistol range before the others cut loose you'll have a runnin' start. It's the best I can do without gettin' myself killed."

Jake nodded his head slightly. "Alright," he said weakly.

"The name's Dan Palliser. Who knows, maybe someday you'll get the chance to return the favor."

Jake tried to focus his attention on watching for the slide Palliser had mentioned, and it seemed slow in coming. The grade grew gradually steeper, and he began to think maybe he'd missed it.

"This ain't good," Palliser said quietly.

Jake looked up and saw that Adler had reined in and was waiting for them to catch up.

"What's keepin' you?" he demanded.

"This big lunk of a geldin' don't lead too good," Palliser lied. "He's comin' along better now."

"I see our bronc stomper's come around," Adler said, an evil light in his eyes. His lips were cracked and swollen, and a trickle of fresh blood mingled with the dried blood and mud in his sparse beard. He turned his horse broadside to Jake's, blocking the trail. Jake's gelding came to a stop and the two men sat staring at each other in a moment of bleak silence. Adler rolled his chew in his cheek, then without warning, spat a thick stream of tobacco juice square into Jake's face. Jake's head snapped back and to the side as he tried to blink the sting from his eyes, instinctively attempting to pull his hands to his face.

Adler laughed, and then grinning wickedly he said, "I gut shot that bay horse. He was still kickin' when we left, but I'm sure he's dead by now."

Jake looked at Adler through squinting eyes but said nothing.

After a moment Adler turned to Palliser and said cheerfully, "Well, we best get movin'. Sooner we can get out o' this rain the better."

Jake's spirits sunk as they moved out and Adler settled in beside him on the downhill side. They came to a slight bend in the trail, and straight ahead Jake saw a wide gap in the tree tops. He guessed this would be the slide Palliser had mentioned, and though his wrists were still bound, he clenched his teeth and put the spurs to Big Jake. The horse took off like he'd been shot from a gun. Adler was screaming and then they were over the edge as a shot split the air.

Instantly Jake knew he'd guessed wrong. There was no slide before him, and he'd launched himself over a six foot drop. Directly ahead and below was a tangle of bleached and boney branches, reaching up like a palisade from the gnarled trunk of a blown down pine. He took in the hopeless scene in an instant, but it seemed an eternity that Big Jake was airborne, hurtling forward and down, and he prayed that they would have enough momentum to clear the barricade. The big gelding's front feet were over, and Jake leaned back, bracing his tied wrists on the pommel against what would be a bone jarring landing. He felt and heard the horse's back feet hit the branches at the same moment another shot rang out. Big Jake's hind end twisted sideways and then they hit the shale below with an impact that drove Jake forward, snapping the cords that bound his wrists. He managed to grab a fistful of mane, fighting to keep his weight back as the gelding fought courageously to gain his footing. Loose stones rattled down the slope as the sound of angry shots hammered out behind, racketing off the canyon walls. Big Jake hadn't quite found his feet when another blow down loomed ahead. In one awkward lurching motion they were up and over, buck-jumping down the impossible slope, weaving around and through a tangled maze of boulders, stumps and dead-fall. It was all Jake could do to stay in the saddle while the brave horse fought to keep his feet, the momentum of the down-hill charge making each laboured stride longer and more out of control.

Somehow they made the bottom of the grade, and as the terrain levelled off to a rock strewn flat before the river, Jake knew something was wrong. The gelding seemed unable to stop his forward motion, and in grunting uneven strides, was valiantly trying to make a wide turn before they went over the bank. With each stride the horse pitched further and further forward, and then his head and chest smashed into the ground. Jake was thrown clear, hitting hard and tumbling wild and out of control before slamming into the trunk of tree. He screamed out at the blinding flash of pure pain, and he rolled over on his back grasping his side and gasping for air. Then he heard it, a wheezing, pain-wracked groan from his big gelding. Jake turned, and struggling to his knees saw the horse lying on his side about twenty feet away. As he watched, Big Jake lifted his heavy head, got his front feet under him and tried to rise.

He couldn't push off, because his left back leg was broken just below the hock, and was flopping grotesquely from side to side. The horse gave a mighty shudder, moaned and fell back to the ground.

Jake didn't remember getting to his feet, but he was staggering trancelike toward the horse, while far above a chorus of gunshots swelled in unison, and he didn't care. He tripped, fell to his knees and then he was crawling. He reached the horse, and it lifted its head again in a feeble attempt to rise.

"No fella, no fella. Just lay still. That's a boy."

Jake put a knee on the gelding's neck and placed a gentle hand on his forehead. The guns above were silent now, and the big horse seemed to draw comfort from the man, though his breathing was ragged and pitiful. Jake stroked his neck and continued speaking in soothing tones while the slanting rain beat down on his bare head and shoulders. He turned and watched the horse's heaving ribs, and then he saw that Big Jake had taken a bullet. His abdomen had been punctured low down and to the side, and a twisted tangle of shiny entrails had spilled out onto the ground. Jake looked quickly away, and then silent tears filled his eyes.

"You're the best, Big Jake. You're the best ever. God I'm sorry."

Jake straightened up and reached into his front pocket for his clasp knife. He kept his knee on the horse's neck, and the gelding lay in quiet trust and submission while Jake cut his throat and watched his life blood pulse out and spread across the cold, wet ground.

—⚞—

From high above, Barry's four riders watched as Jake got back to his feet. He stood a moment over the dead horse, then turned and walked drunkenly downstream to disappear into the timber. Adler began to curse bitterly as the three other men mounted up. For his part, Palliser couldn't help but be moved by the horse thief's blatant disregard for their fire, as he did the right thing. *The right thing.* Palliser shook his head involuntarily, and felt suddenly small, used up and dirty.

The loose horses were gone from sight up the trail, spooked by the shooting, and the rain was showing no signs of letting up. Adler was pacing back and forth at the edge of the cliff, determined to find a way to get their horses down, but there was none. Cursing again, he turned to mount up, and then he saw Palliser's rifle in its scabbard.

"Dan! You got a rifle!"

Palliser nodded.

"Why didn't you use it?!"

"Slipped my mind I reckon."

With his hands on his hips, Adler stood and regarded Palliser with smoldering eyes. Then he said quietly, "Funny thing how your horse bumped into mine and spoiled my first shot."

"Careful, Adler. Don't say something you'll wish you never had."

"I'll say whatever I please an' make you like it!" Adler snarled back through clenched teeth.

The rain was a steady curtain of sound, and Adler's horse snorted as he bobbed his head, pawing the ground impatiently. Both men faced each other in a tense and silent stand-off, and then Palliser spoke.

"Spit it out, Adler. Just remember, I never met that horse thief before today, so why would I care a lick what happens to him. If you think it's worth a killin' though, you can cut loose anytime."

Adler felt the coiled tension slowly leave him. He was sure he could kill Palliser any time he wanted to, but there was that hint of caution that told him a man didn't reach Palliser's age in this line of work unless he was good at his business. Taylor gave him an out.

"If we don't catch up with them ponies before they hit them meadows on the downhill they're surely gonna scatter."

Adler looked at him, and nodded. "But what do we do about the horse thief?" he said bitterly.

Palliser took the opportunity to get back on side. "The way I see it, it don't much matter whether he's dead or alive. He's out of it." Adler turned back to face Palliser, who continued speaking. "Once we get back an' Sheriff Kingman puts up his reward dodgers, why would he stick around? I doubt he's willin' to go to prison for somethin' he never did, and even if he wanted to stay in the country, whose gonna believe his side of the story?"

Adler thought a moment then admitted reluctantly, "You're probably right, but it galls me not to kill him after what he done."

"Well, there's that slide about a quarter mile ahead," Palliser suggested. "You could probably get your horse down to the river there. I could lend you my rifle, but you'd be huntin' him on foot. You'd never get your horse through that tangled mess of bush along the creek."

Adler swore, then turned and looked down the hill. "Forget it," he snapped. "Let's go find them ponies. I'm sick o' this rain. I'm for spendin' the night in the cabin on Pine Creek and bringin' them back tomorrow." He mounted up, and the other riders fell in behind him, moving up the trail in a soggy trot.

—⁓—

Jake hadn't gone far into the timber before he fell to his knees and retched violently. His head began to swim, and he lay down with his face to the rain. For a while it was hard to care enough about anything to bother trying to rise, and then he remembered his horse, fighting and willing himself forward with a bullet in his belly long enough to carry him out of pistol range, and he got to his feet. Beyond that, he couldn't seem to focus on anything, but it was enough.

For a short time he stumbled aimlessly through the trees, but then his mind began to work more clearly. He had no idea how far they'd come from the Two Canyons cabin, but what he did know was that he needed a horse. What had Palliser said? *"A horse thief on the run serves our purpose as good as a dead one."* Well, he wasn't going to run. He didn't give it much thought, and maybe he was being a fool, but he made the decision and would stubbornly see it through. He had no idea what the purpose was that Palliser spoke of, but again he reasoned it had something to do with the cattle on the mesa.

Jake stopped under the heavy boughs of old forest pine to catch his breath. He'd gradually climbed up and away from the river where the undergrowth was thick and tangled, and soon found the going easier. He came to the realization, how-ever, that he had to go back to his horse, as he'd be needing his saddle. He reasoned that if Barry's gunmen were looking for him they wouldn't expect this, and if he stayed high, they just might pass beneath him. He'd need to move with caution, but when it came right down to it, he had no choice. The only saddle horses available to him were the colts back at the cabin, and he didn't feel up to trying any of them bareback. There was a good chance he'd be putting on some hard miles in the days to come, and for that he'd need his saddle. With his mind made up, he turned and started back.

When he reached the break in the trees, he was well above his dead gelding. He looked down at the lifeless form of Big Jake, his gray coat dark with the rain and horribly still. Nothing moved on the cold gray slopes, and the only sound was the constant rain and the churning river. For a moment Jake lost his forward momentum, his spirit sinking to the bleakness of his surroundings and he was too tired to fight it. Then he turned his face slowly away and took one heavy step, then another. Keeping to the cover of the trees, he made a slow labouring climb back up the hill. He reached the top and was able to scramble up the cliff face to find the trail was empty; the ground churned by the horses a wet, shiny ribbon against the washed grass. He took a chance and stepped out into the open, and after briefly studying the tracks realized all four riders had followed the loose horses. Not knowing how soon they'd be back, he made his way as quickly as possible back down to his gelding.

He had to undo his cinches on the off side, and it took quite an effort to wrestle the stirrup out from under the horse. When it finally came free he sat back, breathing heavily, fresh pain tearing at his ribs. After a time, he got wearily to his feet and gently slipped the bridle off Big Jake's head. Dark blood coated the throat latch, and he wiped it clean on the wet grass, then turned and made his way back up the hill without looking back. He didn't bother with cover, but sought the best footing and the easiest way, frustrated at his weakness, only able to make a few yards at a time before having to drop his saddle and rest. When he finally reached the trail, he hid his saddle in some junipers, and too tired for caution, turned and headed back down the trail.

Jake walked for an hour, and the path he followed was now almost level with the creek. A short time later the stream turned sharply, spilling into a larger river, boiling brown and muddy with the runoff. Not far ahead in the failing light, he could see the country opened up a little, and half an hour after that, he broke free of the timber. The first thing he saw was the wide dark mouth of the Two Canyons, and turning, saw the cabin and corrals down the slope below. He suddenly realized it was no longer raining, and to the north, a feeble ray of light found its way through a break in the clouds. He picked up his pace as he headed for the buildings, and seeing the blood bay in the pasture behind the cabin, was relieved to know Palliser had spoken the truth. He decided then that this was the horse he would ride. The colt came over to the fence as he walked by on his way to the barn, and then Jake kicked something in the mud. Looking down he saw the crushed form of his hat, and stooping to pick it up, knocked the crown back into shape before carefully easing it onto his head. The bay colt was still watching him and Jake smiled grimly.

"Well big fella," he said. "You ready to go to work?"

He studied the horse a moment, and then decided he didn't have the strength to lead him back up to his saddle. He was going to attempt the trip bareback. With a new sense of determination he turned for the barn to get a bridle. He paused at the door to look down at the over-turned wagon and the flooded river crossing. It was hard to believe it was only this morning that he had ridden with Lee-two back to the home ranch. He shook his head and stepped inside.

It was dark in the barn, but habit and memory guided him and he had little trouble finding a bridle. Next he went to the cabin, but his pistol and shell belt that had hung by his bed were gone. No doubt Adler had planned to plant them on him after he'd been killed to make his story more believable. Stepping back outside, he headed for the horse pasture. Both the bay and the filly walked to meet him, and he had no trouble slipping the bridle on the bay. With his ribs hurting the way they were, he knew he'd have a hard time swinging up, so he led the colt through the gate and then alongside the rail fence.

He paused a moment, then said quietly, "Well God, I reckon I'm gonna need some help here. I know for a fact that you're the Lord of the beasts of the field, and I'd sure appreciate it if you told this boy to behave."

The break in the clouds had spread along the horizon to the west, and the day's fading glory turned the puddles on the ground to golden light. Jake placed his left hand that gripped the reins firmly on the colt's withers, and with his right hand resting on his hind quarter, stepped up onto the second rail. The horse stood solid and still, and then Jake summoned his strength, lifted his belly onto the colt's back, and awkwardly swung his right leg over. The horse side stepped nervously, but then stood quiet. Jake breathed a sigh of relief.

"Thank you," he said. Reaching forward he scratched the gelding on the neck. "You got big shoes to fill there, mister.

I got a feelin' if there's a horse that could do it though, it just might be you."

After a brief pause, Jake kneed the horse forward, and the gelding moved out willingly up the hill and away from the cabin.

X

Lee-two's eyes came open, and she wondered what it was that had awakened her. The wind had picked up outside, and there was the familiar tap tap of the lilac bush against the window. She was sure it wasn't this, as it was a sound that had become so familiar it was almost a comfort. Then she heard it again, a low but persistent knocking on the back door.

"Father!" she whispered into the darkness, but his slow, steady breathing was uninterrupted. She heard the latch move, and then the sound of the wind outside grew louder as the door swung open.

"Father!" she said again, only more loudly as fear gripped her. Her father stirred in his bed, and then she heard a half spoken whisper.

"Chickadee, it's me, don't be afraid."

"Jake?"

"Yes, don't light a lamp."

Lee-two scrambled out of bed, pulling off a blanket which she wrapped tightly around herself, and then she heard her father's voice in the darkness.

"What is it?"

"Mr. Sullivan is here! Don't light the lamp!" Without waiting for a reply she hurried out of the bedroom. Jake had closed the door, and she saw his dark shape loom before her. Stepping close she asked, "Jake? What is wrong?" Lee-two was unaware that she'd used his first name for the second time, and then she heard her father come into the room.

"Sorry to bother you," Jake said. "I hope you don't mind."

"No mind," Lee-one's voice came out of the darkness, "someting is wrong?"

Jake sighed and then said, "It's a long story, and I don't even know the half of it, so it's hard to know where to start. There's big trouble though and I'm in the middle of it. I don't want to drag you into it, but I need a bite to eat and a place to rest for a couple of hours. I'll be gone before daylight."

Lee-two could hear the weakness in Jake's voice, and she said quickly, "Here, there is a chair by the wall. Please, sit down. Do not worry, Mr. Sullivan, you are welcome anytime."

"Thank you, ma'am," Jake said as he sunk wearily into the chair, "but I'll need to leave pretty quick. Daylight's only a couple hours off an' I just tied my horse back by the outhouse. He'll give me away sure."

"Do not worry, Mr. Sullivan. There is a little meadow back in the trees where Mrs. Daniels kept her milk cow. No one ever goes there. I will move Big Jake for you while father gets you something to eat."

"Big Jake is dead."

Lee-two gasped, and after a moment of troubled silence she whispered, "Oh no! What is happening?"

Jake hesitated, and then said, "Maybe, you and your pa should find a chair. It'll take some time, but I'll tell you what I know."

"First you eat," Lee-one said firmly. "I have sowa dough biscuit and cole bean."

"Thank you. That would be great."

"Are you thirsty?" Lee-two asked. "I could get you some water."

"Please," Jake said. "I'm very thirsty."

When Jake finished speaking, a hint of gray light showed in the windows. Both Lee-one and Lee-two insisted that since they would soon be getting up anyway, he should take one of the beds in the bedroom. Jake's protests were quickly brushed aside, and after reminding them to wake him in an hour, he fell onto Lee-two's bed and was soon dead to the world.

Lee-two kindled the fire in the cook stove, and then took a seat at the small table across from her father. Speaking softly in her native tongue she asked, "Are you afraid?"

"A little."

"What are you afraid of?"

Lee-one didn't answer right away, and then he said, "I know we do the right thing. How could I not help the man who saved the life of my little bird? Yet even if it were not so, I know that this is what my Lord would have me do. Still I am afraid. It seems that every time I think we will soon be going back to China, something happens."

"Maybe God does not want us to go back to China," Lee-two said.

"Ah, my little bird. This also I am afraid of. I am not blind. I can see how your heart shines in your eyes every time you speak of this man, Mr. Suwivan, and now that he is here, even in this difficult situation, you cannot hide your happiness."

Lee-two was silent for a while, and then she said, "Mr. Sullivan is a kind man, father."

"I know he is a kind man. But as you say, he is kind even to his horse. He was kind to a Chinese boy when he jumped into the river, not a beautiful young woman. I am afraid you will mistake this kindness for something else. In China, there are many who think they are far better than the foreigners. It is the same everywhere I think. I know this to be true in America. We are Chinese. We are the foreigners here."

Again Lee-two was silent, and it was Lee-one who broke the silence.

"What are you thinking, my little bird?"

Lee-two looked across the table at her father, and even in the semi-darkness he could see there were tears in her eyes.

"Even if there is pain to follow," she said. "I will not let it steal the happiness I feel now."

Lee-one smiled sadly at her. "You get more beautiful every day," he said. "More and more like your mother every day. I keep praying that God will make these cowboys blind. Maybe there is one cowboy He will give eyes to see."

Lee-two smiled. "Thank you, father," she said softly. "I will go move this cowboy's horse now."

"There is no one around but the blacksmith and the injured man they brought from town," Lee-one said. "I think we should let Mr. Suwivan sleep."

"I think that is a good idea," Lee-two said as she rose to her feet. She turned quickly and headed out the back door.

Jake woke from a groggy sleep to the sound of a lazy fly buzzing against the window pane. His head felt thick and his mouth was dry, and for a moment he had no idea where he was. Sunlight streamed through the window and there was movement in the next room; then he remembered. He sat up quickly, and the pain in his side made him gasp involuntarily. He heard a chair scrape on the floor and the sound of quick footsteps, and then Lee-two came through the door.

"I hope you don't mind," she said. "We thought you needed the sleep."

"What about my horse?" Jake asked, swinging his feet to the floor. "I can't let them find me here."

"I moved your horse while it was still dark," Lee-two said, taking a seat on her father's bed. "There is no one around so I am sure it will be okay. I hope you are not angry."

Jake shook his head, and then lay back down on the bed. "No," he said. "I'd just hate to bring trouble on you, that's all. I probably shouldn't have come."

"Where else could you go?" Lee-two asked. "I am glad you came. Remember, you promised me a visit."

Jake smiled. "That seems like a month ago."

"Can I get you anything?" Lee-two asked. "Are you hungry?"

"You don't have to wait on me, Lee-two," Jake said. "I'm afraid I'm bein' an awful bother."

"You are not a bother, and you need to rest. What can I get for you?"

"Water would be good. I'm powerful dry."

Lee-two got to her feet and left the room. When she returned, Jake rose up on one elbow and took the cup she offered him.

The water was deliciously cool, and as he gulped it down, Lee-two gasped, "Mr. Sullivan! Your head! You have an awful gash!"

Jake set the cup on the floor. "I reckon that's where Palliser whacked me with his pistol," he said, reaching up to carefully feel the welt on his head.

"You did not mention this last night."

"No, I might have left that part out." Jake agreed.

"Let me look at it," Lee-two said. "This must be cared for."

"Oh, I'm sure it's alright. I got a pretty thick skull."

"Please, Mr. Sullivan. Sit up and let me look at it."

Jake obediently swung his feet to the floor and Lee-two stepped up beside him. He felt her deft fingers move through his hair along the wound, and he was aware of her closeness.

"I will need to clean this," she said. "I will be right back."

Lee-two left quickly, and Jake heard her busily moving around in the other room. She returned shortly with a basin of water and some rags. Placing the basin on the floor, she knelt down and dipped the rags, then straightened to stand directly in front of him.

"I will try to be gentle," she said. "Please tell me if I am hurting you."

Jake nodded and leaned forward, his elbows on his knees. He winced slightly as Lee-two pressed the damp rag against his scalp, but in spite of the fresh pain, the water and Lee-two's gentle probing fingers had a soothing effect. She pushed his head slightly down and forward as she worked her way further back behind his ear. Once again, Jake was conscious of her closeness and her clean, fresh smell, and though it made him a little uncomfortable, he didn't want to move.

Lee-two stepped back, kneeled and dipped her rags in the basin. Smiling up at him she said, "I think you must have a thick skull, Mr. Sullivan. It is good that you do I think. That is a very bad wound."

Jake didn't reply, and Lee-two rose and pulled his head close as she continued bathing his scalp. Jake heard the front door of the cabin come open, and he straightened self-consciously, but Lee-two stopped him with a firm hand on the back of his head.

"Please, I am not quite finished," she said.

Jake let his head fall forward again, and if Lee-two was the least bit uncomfortable when her father came into the room, she showed no outward sign. Jake wasn't sure Lee-one felt the same way when he stopped short in the doorway.

"Mr. Sullivan has a bad wound on his head," Lee-two said, turning to face her father. "Could you please bring me some clean water?"

Lee-one hesitated briefly, crossed the floor and picked up the basin. Without a word he turned and walked stiffly from the room. Jake was suddenly aware that Lee-two was humming softly while she worked, and he knew then without a doubt that he loved her. He glanced quickly up, but she was focused on the task at hand and didn't notice. Lee-one returned with the basin of water, set it on the floor, and after an awkward pause left the room.

Jake was disappointed when Lee-two stepped back from him and said, "I think that will be much better."

Jake nodded, "Thanks."

"I will get a clean cloth for a bandage, and then I will change the pillow case."

Jake glanced down and saw blood stains where his head had lain. "Sorry. I didn't realize…"

Lee-two didn't hear him as she had turned to leave the room. Jake sat where he was, unsure of what to do. He could hear the clink of dishes and muffled conversation, and then Lee-two returned.

She smiled at him, and while she wrapped his head, she said, "Father is heating up some stew. I am sure you must be hungry."

"Yes, ma'am."

"I think it probably is best if you sleep some more after you have eaten. It will help you to get your strength back."

"I feel pretty used up, that's for sure. I hope I ain't bein' a bother."

Lee-two smiled sincerely. "I am glad you are here, Mr. Sullivan. We are taking turns you see."

Jake smiled. "I suppose we are," he said. "I just hope no one finds my horse."

"There is no one around. Everything will be fine."

Lee-one came to the door. "Stew weddy," he said.

Jake followed Lee-two into the other room. He noticed there were two chairs pulled up to the small table by the front door, and that the third chair was a stump that had seen time as a chopping block. He quickly chose the stump, and as he was sitting down Lee-one said, "No, no. You guest."

"This is fine, Lee-one," Jake responded. "You two use your regular chairs."

Lee-one stubbornly insisted. Smiling politely and gesturing with his good arm he said again, "No, please. You guest, please."

"Please take the chair, Mr. Sullivan," Lee-two said. "We are honored to have you as a guest. My father wants to give you our best."

Jake nodded, and reluctantly got to his feet and took the chair across from Lee-two. When he was seated, Lee-one sat down, and with both hands on his lap, bowed his head.

"Tank you Heavenly Fawda foe many plessing. Tank you you spaya Mr. Suwivan life. Tank you foe you caya and potection. Pless owa food, guide owa way. Amen."

For the most part, the meal was eaten in silence, with Lee-one making a few awkward attempts at conversation. Lee-two was not near as talkative as she had been at the Two Canyons cabin, but as far as Jake could tell, she was feeling comfortable and relaxed. He took her relative silence to be a natural deferral to her father as head of the house. Jake felt surprisingly unsure of himself, and he knew it came with his realization of how he felt about Lee-two, and his not knowing what to do about it.

They were almost finished eating when they were startled by Cliff Barry's rasping voice outside, followed by a hard knocking on the door. Jake rose quickly, and snatching his plate from the table, stepped back as the door swung open. With his back against the wall, and only the open door between himself and Barry, he held his breath and waited.

"Lee-one! I got four hungry riders out here. I need you to throw something together and make it quick!"

Before Lee-one could reply, the door slammed shut and Barry was gone. Jake stood facing a startled Lee-one and Lee-two, who were still seated.

Lee-one got to his feet, and showing complete composure said, "Awmose bad. Tank you Jesus."

Jake looked at the three cups on the table and his scattered cutlery, and breathed a sigh of relief. "I'm glad he was in a hurry," he said.

Lee-two rose and came to stand beside him. "I am glad you were quick to act," she said. "We will be gone awhile, but no one ever comes in here. You should get some rest."

"I need to get out of here," Jake said. "All I need is for my horse to whinny and give me away. I don't want to get you and your father in trouble."

Lee-two looked up at him, and here brown eyes were gentle and peaceful. "I am not afraid," she said. "You must wait till dark. Is there anything you need?"

Jake hesitated a moment, then said, "I'll need a gun."

Lee-two's eyes grew sober. "I will tell my father," she said.

XI

The afternoon passed slowly, and though Jake tried, he was unable to sleep. Now and then he heard voices outside, and he was sure more of the Anchor D riders had returned. He paced the floor like a caged animal, restless and anxious. The knowledge that his horse was just a hundred yards behind the cabin waiting to be discovered was a constant nagging irritation that would not let go. He second guessed himself time and time again, thinking he should maybe brave the daylight and make a break for it, then deciding to lay low and wait for the cover of darkness. Finally he was able to resign himself to his situation, and sitting on the bed while the shadows lengthened, settled into patient silence.

The front door came open, and Jake's head lifted and he waited. He heard it close, and then there was the sound of light footsteps. He got to his feet as Lee-two came to the bedroom door. She handed him a Colt 45, and said. "I must hurry back. Several of the men are here."

Jake felt the weight of the pistol and spun the cylinder. "Where did you get this?" he asked.

"My father gave it to me. I do not know where he got it. Jake, you must listen to me. There is much to tell."

Jake shoved the pistol in his waist band and looked at Lee-two. "What is it?" he asked.

"Remember I told you Mr. Barry does not think I understand English?"

Jake nodded. "Yes I remember."

"He talked very freely with a man I have never seen before. I was washing the tables and they were the only ones in the room. I do not like this man."

"What did he look like?" Jake asked.

"He was tall and thin with yellow hair. His eyes told me that he is a cruel man."

"Adler," Jake said quietly.

"Do you know him?"

Jake nodded. "He's one of the fella's that tried to kill me. Is he still here?"

"No. He left early with Nathan and another man. They are going to town to tell the sheriff about the stolen horses."

Jake nodded his head. "Figures," he said. "I reckon I'll have my name on some reward dodgers shortly. So what was Barry tellin' Adler?"

"He said Carmody was getting impatient because Nathan had not been in for over a week. He said they were running out of time and told this man to make sure he got Nathan good and drunk and got him to the tables. Then this man asked Mr. Barry, 'Why don't you just kill him?' and Mr. Barry said it might come to that."

Jake looked intently at Lee-two, a question on his brow. "I wonder what that's all about?" he said.

"I don't know, but I thought I should tell you."

Jake was silent, and he looked out the window at the gathering darkness.

"The sheriff will be looking for you?" Lee-two asked.

Jake nodded.

"You will be gone when I come back?"

Again Jake nodded. "Yes," he said.

Lee-two was silent a moment, then she asked hesitantly, "Will you be going far away?"

Jake looked quickly back at her, and then shook his head. "No. I'm gonna stick around. I want to get to the bottom of this so I can clear my name. I don't want to have to leave this country."

Lee-two put a tentative hand on his sleeve and said, "I will pray for your safety." Then without another word she turned and walked quickly out the front door.

"So when did you boys start ridin' for the Anchor D?" young Daniels asked.

"We were workin' for an outfit south o' here an' lookin' to see some new country," Adler responded. "We met up with Barry when him an' Cob were combin' the breaks along the river. They were shorthanded, so here we are." Adler turned in his saddle and began digging in his saddle bags. He produced a half empty whiskey bottle, took a swig, and then offered it to Daniels. "I guess you boys had better luck with your gather."

Daniels took the bottle and nodded. "A bunch of the basin outfits are roundin' up too, so it helps. I sure can't figure why we're comin' up with such a short count though." Daniels took a drink, wiped his mouth with the back of his hand, and then offered the bottle to Palliser. When Palliser declined, Daniels handed it back to Adler.

"I reckon we better take it easy on this 'till after we see the sheriff." Adler said. "I figure we'll have time to make up for it later."

Daniels didn't answer, and his thoughts returned to Jake Sullivan. He'd been shocked and strangely disappointed when he heard about Jake stealing the horses and he wondered why. The man had admitted to being a horse thief, so why should he care? Yet he'd been in a bleak and foul mood since the morning, and he found himself looking forward to a good drunk. He felt cheated somehow, and he realized he'd enjoyed his time at Two Canyons more than he'd enjoyed anything for a long time, and inexplicably, had started to see the Anchor D in a different light. He'd actually begun to take an interest in how the roundup was going, but this morning had decided he didn't care. With that decision, however, came an unwelcome emptiness. He stole a glance at Adler, and unconsciously shook his head. Barry had definitely hired a couple of beauties with these two. He wondered why, and then decided he didn't care about that either.

"Hand me that bottle, Adler," he said. "I'd like to have another pull."

Adler fetched the bottle, and Daniels tipped it back.

"Take it easy young fella," Palliser said. "The reason Barry sent you was 'cause you know the sheriff."

Daniels looked at Palliser, his eyes watering and his belly burning. The whiskey had already dulled his caution, and he said, "You afraid he might have your picture on his wall or somethin'?"

Palliser looked levelly at him a moment, then answered quietly, "Could be," he said.

Daniels put the cork back in the bottle and handed it to Adler, and for a while they rode in silence. The sun was behind the hills when they saw the town of Utica ahead.

"Probably best if you an' Daniels go see the sheriff," Adler said. "I'll wait for you at the barn."

"Alright," Palliser said.

Jake carefully removed the bandage from his head before gingerly putting on his hat. He drew the pistol from his waistband, checked the loads, and then sat on the edge of the bed while darkness slowly took the room. When he felt sure it was time, he moved to the back door and quietly stepped out into the evening. He paused in the deep shadows by the cabin and looked up toward the big house. Light showed in a single window and he hesitated, wondering if there might not be a weak link in Barry's plans, then he turned and found the path behind the outhouse. His horse nickered softly at his approach, and then Jake stumbled into an old page wire fence grown in with grass. He found a walking gate a few feet to the south, and lying on the ground just outside the gate was the dark hulk of his saddle. He stooped to pick it up and heard a light clinking sound as something fell to the ground. He stooped again, felt around and found his cinch. Straightening up he smiled, realizing Lee-two must have un-done every strap and buckle she could find when unsaddling his horse. *Good thing I don't need to make a quick get-away*, he thought, as he forced the gate open against a tangle of old grass.

Once saddled, Jake led his horse out of the small pasture and mounted up. He paused a moment, then instead of riding north toward town, he turned south and clung to the shadows of a poplar bluff, skirting the compound and climbing the gentle slope up toward the big house. The windows were all dark now, and dismounting, Jake tied his horse at the edge of the trees, stepped over a low picket fence and made his way to the back door. Quietly he climbed the steps, drew his pistol and then tried the latch. As he suspected, the door was not locked. It creaked on its hinges as he slowly swung it open and the sound was loud in the stillness. A burst of laughter erupted from down by the cookhouse, and Jake stepped quickly inside, closing the door behind him. He waited, tense and listening, but all was still. Presently his eyes grew accustomed to the darkness, and he saw that he was standing in a good-sized kitchen. To his left was an open door to what he guessed would be a pantry, and across the room and directly in front of him was another door. Before going any further, he bent down, set his gun on the floor and removed his spurs, stuffing one in each hip pocket. Picking up the pistol, he straightened up and slowly made his way across the floor.

The next room was a sitting room, and on the left side, rising up from the entry way, Jake saw a heavy wooden banister. He guessed the bedrooms would be upstairs, but as he crossed the carpeted floor, he heard the low and even sound of someone snoring. At the foot of the stairs, and just across from the entry way was another door, and Jake reasoned that because Abe Daniels was crippled, he would likely avoid using the stairs, preferring to sleep on the main floor. He paused briefly, then put his hand on the door and it swung freely. The sound of Abe's snoring was uninterrupted, and Jake quietly stepped into the bedroom.

Abe Daniels was lying on his back, his face relaxed in sleep, and by the faint light from a widow over the bed Jake could see a wooden chair with pants draped over the back. He sat down on the chair, hesitated a moment, then shoved the barrel of his pistol against Abe's temple. Abe's eyes came instantly open.

"Keep quiet," Jake said sternly.

Abe slowly turned his head. "Who are you?" he demanded, his eyes showing more anger than fear.

"The horse thief," Jake answered.

Abe's eyes went from Jake's gun to his face.

"You heard of me, I reckon," Jake said.

"Barry was in earlier," Abe responded.

"Ah, Clifford Barry. Your trusted foreman."

"What are you doin' here?" Abe demanded.

Jake didn't answer immediately, but after a pause said, "What are *you* doin' here, that's the real question."

Abe looked at Jake, clearly taken aback by his answer. "What am I doin' here? I own this place!" he growled.

"For how long?" Jake asked.

"What are you talkin' about?"

Jake looked hard and straight into Abe's eyes, and then said suddenly and unexpectedly, "Your wife was no good, I reckon."

With a deep throated growl, Abe came off the bed and Jake rose quickly to stand above him, pressing the barrel of his pistol hard against Abe's chest and forcing him back down onto his pillow. Abe glared up at him, and Jake said through clenched teeth, "So I was wrong about your wife. Why in heaven's name then, do you treat her son like a worthless cast-off? Why would you build this place up just to leave it to Barry? He hates the son she bore you! Why do *you* show so little faith in your own flesh and blood?"

Abe Daniels looked away, his eyes hard but troubled. Looking back to Jake he said quietly, "You don't know anything."

"No, you don't know anything. You're too busy hidin' out up here feelin' sorry for yourself to see past your nose."

"What do you want?" Abe asked thickly.

"I want you to think about a few things, then maybe you'll realize you ain't dead yet and you'll get off your back long enough to do some good around here."

Abe Daniels was angry, but there was a curious ring of truth in what Jake said and it troubled him. He looked past the pistol into Jake's eyes. "What things?" he asked.

"For starters, how come your foreman's got a jag of cattle up on the mesa at Two Canyons that he don't want you to know about? How come when I found out about them cattle he thought it necessary to cook up this horse stealin' yarn to get me out of the way? Why was he willin' to go so far as to have one of his hardcase crew beef me to make sure I stayed out of the way? Then ask yourself how come Barry's in thick with some saloon owner in Utica, and why do the both of 'em do everything in their power to keep your boy drunk an' pilin' up a gamblin' debt? Speakin' of a hardcase crew, how come your cook's daughter has to pretend to be a boy 'cause she's afraid of what might happen to her if they knew she was a girl? What kind of an outfit are you runnin' here anyway? Oh sorry, I forgot. You ain't runnin' it. You're leavin' that in the capable hands of a foreman who hates your son and is tryin' to steal you blind."

"You're talkin' nonsense," Abe said gruffly.

"Am I?" Jake responded. "I reckon if you use your head, keep your mouth shut an' your eyes open over the next couple of days you might think different. Anyway, I gotta go. I don't think Nathan's got any idea what he's up against and he might be in trouble." Jake stood and regarded Abe Daniels a moment, and Abe returned his stare.

"Nice meetin' you," Jake said finally, and then he turned for the door. As he was leaving the room he turned back to face Daniels. "I shouldn't have told you about Lee-two bein' a girl. I promised her I'd keep it a secret. You may be a coward, but I reckon you're a gentleman."

Jake left the room and moments later Abe heard the back door close. He stayed where he was and stared at the ceiling. The horse thief's words went round and round in his head, and he doubted most of it was true. Two things he realized were true, however, were that the horse thief believed in his son, and that he himself was a coward. He had no use for a coward and he wished he could believe in his son.

Jake glanced back toward the house as he reached his horse. No lights showed and all was quiet. He guessed Abe had decided not to sound the alarm, which was one thing he'd been afraid he might do. It was a good sign that maybe his talk had done some good. Though he'd thought it necessary to crowd the man and didn't regret doing it, he remembered his part of the conversation with distaste. Mounting up, he retraced his steps from half an hour earlier. A welcome light reached out to him from the Lee's cabin, and he paused momentarily then rode a wide circle and took the dark trail to Utica.

XII

The hills to the south and west of town were washed in the light of a moon that would soon be rising, while the valley and the town of Utica waited in darkness. Palliser sat on a stump chair in the deep shadows under the awning of the Claybrook Hotel. Ragged ruts full of water gave back the light that spilled through the open doors of Carmody's Saloon, two doors down and across the deserted street. Palliser knew Adler was expecting him, but he stayed where he was. He was unsure exactly what was going on and equally unsure who was giving the orders, Barry or Carmody. He had the feeling though that each man believed himself in charge. It came to him now that one of the things he liked the least about his line of work was the company he had to keep, and he'd had about enough of Adler's. To be fair, he'd had about enough of his own as well. He was trying to remember why he was here, and nothing added up. Was it the money? He'd get paid well he knew, but it wouldn't last. He'd soon be broke and looking for work again. Work? Could you call it work? His past was a shadowy trail of faceless men who'd paid him to do the things they didn't have the guts to do themselves. Time and again he'd risked his life for men who would want to forget him as quickly as possible, just as he would forget them.

"I'm nothin'," he said out loud. "Nothin'."

He came to the slow realization that he was finished. He had no idea where he would go, but he didn't have the stomach to stay where he was. He hadn't been paid, but he didn't care. That was just it he realized. He didn't care. He was empty.

"Nothin'," he said again.

The sound of a lone horse splashing up the street caught his attention. He looked to the deeper darkness at the edge of town and at first saw nothing. Then a white blaze and presently a horse and rider materialized out of the gloom. There was something familiar about the rider, and then it hit him. It was the horse thief! Palliser sat tense and still, wondering why the man didn't have the sense to get out of the country. As he watched, the horse thief drew to a stop in front of Carmody's, studied the door a moment, then stiffly dismounted to tie his horse and mount the steps to the saloon. As he entered the front door, Palliser came off his stump chair, ducked under the hitch rail and ran kitty corner across the muddy street.

Jake pulled his hat brim down over his eyes, reached to feel the pistol in his waistband, then stepped through the door of Carmody's Saloon. The room was crowded with riders from the basin roundup, and no one seemed to take note of his entrance. He moved to the shadows along the wall to survey the room, and immediately spotted Adler. He was seated at a corner table with three other men, his back to the wall, studying the cards in his hand. Directly across from

Adler, sitting with his back to Jake, was Nathan Daniels. Jake paused briefly, and then moved toward the bar on the side wall. He angled toward a vacant space near the far end, and once he reached it, turned quickly on his heel. In three fast strides he was standing feet apart at Adler's table. Adler looked up from his cards, and as the shock of recognition took his face Jake grabbed the edge of the table with both hands and slammed it violently into his chest, pushing him back and pinning him against the wall. Adler's breath was driven from his lungs as bottles and glasses crashed to the floor along with an explosion of cards and money. The other players, save for Daniels, scrambled clear of the table, one man hitting the floor as his chair tipped over backwards.

"Jake, what are you doin' here?" Daniels drawled in a bewildered, whiskey clouded voice. Jake ignored him, and his hot eyes bored into Adler's. Both of Adler's hands were trapped on top of the table; there was no way he could reach his pistol. Jake saw naked fear in the man's eyes, and it was clear the outlaw expected no mercy. Adler's head turned slightly, and for the briefest moment, hope showed on his face before it was masked by a wicked sneer. Palliser had stepped through the side door.

"Well, horse thief," Adler said. "Looks like you got trouble."

Palliser walked forward and stopped a short distance from the table. "You got it wrong," he said quietly. Then, without taking his eyes from Adler, he motioned with his head to Jake and said, "I'm with him."

"Since when?" Adler snarled.

"Jake?" a confused Daniels asked again. "What are you doin' here?"

Ignoring Daniels, and still looking at Adler, Palliser spit out the words, "Since I realized how sick I am of lookin' at you, how sick I am of listenin' to you, and how sick I am of bein' like you. I'm through, Adler. I'm done with the likes of you."

Adler's eyes grew hard with hate, the hint of fear returning as he looked uncertainly from Palliser back to Jake, who said sternly, "Nathan, go get on your horse."

"Are you comin' too?"

"I'll be right behind you."

Nathan rose obediently from his chair and weaved his way toward the door without looking back.

Jake stood and regarded Adler in a bleak moment of silence before muttering through clenched teeth, "This is for Big Jake." With every ounce of strength he had, he drove his right fist square into the man's face. Pain ripped through his side as he fell awkwardly across the table and Adler's head snapped back to hit the wall. Jake straightened and looked first at Adler, slumped unconscious on the table, then at Palliser.

"Meet me in the alley out back." Palliser said evenly.

Jake hesitated, wondering at the wisdom of trusting the man. He glanced again at the slack form of Adler, then back at Palliser, remembering he owed him his life. With a growing sense of urgency he nodded and turned for the front door.

Jake stepped into the night and almost ran into Daniels who was standing aimless and confused on the boardwalk. Seeing Nathan's buckskin a few ponies down on the hitch rail, he grabbed the boy's elbow and roughly guided him down the stairs. Once he had him mounted, Jake took the reins and led the buckskin over to his bay. Before mounting up he looked at Daniels.

"Can you ride?" he asked.

Daniels head came up in surprise. "I can ride anythin' that grows hair, cowboy!" he slurred boastfully.

"Just try not to fall off." Jake winced as he swung into the saddle, and then turned to meet Palliser emerging from the shadows of a narrow side street beside the saloon. Wordlessly, Palliser turned his horse around and again Jake hesitated, then trusting his intuition, he fell in behind. They were headed for the darkness of the alley when Palliser pulled up short.

"Funny," he said, barely above a whisper. "There was a light in that back widow just a moment ago. Turn around. Quick!"

Palliser wheeled his horse, and as Jake followed suit, a bright flash of flame blossomed at the back corner of the saloon, and the hard sound of pistol shots racketed off the clapboard walls on either side. Instinctively, Jake hunched his shoulders, leaning forward in the saddle as his half-broke bay bolted for the open street in an out-of-control runaway. Daniels' reins were ripped from his hands, and his knee smashed into Palliser's as he blew past him, making a wide reckless turn. The bay almost floundered as it hit the deeper churned up mud of the street, but then fought to its feet before pounding down the main street and out of town. Jake didn't bother trying to rein him in but let the horse have its head. The bay was eating up the ground in long glorious strides, and glancing over his shoulder, Jake saw two riders coming on hard behind him. His horse was moving in a relaxed, flowing rhythm now, and Jake slowly brought him to a stop. Palliser pulled alongside, his horse breathing hard, and then had to move quickly off the trail to avoid being run over by Daniels' buckskin. The horse came to a bone-jarring stop, with Daniels hunched forward in the saddle, gripping the horn with both hands. Daniels looked up at Jake and grinned.

"I'm glad you never fell off," Jake said.

"I can ride anythin' that grows hair, cowboy!"

"I reckon maybe you can," Jake agreed, and then he turned to regard Palliser.

Palliser looked at him a moment, then said, "Dan Palliser, we met once before."

"I ain't likely to forget. Jake Sullivan." Jake hesitated a moment, then extended his right hand. Palliser took it and they shook hands firmly.

"I reckon we should pull off the road a ways," Palliser said. "There'll likely be a fast horse headed for the ranch shortly."

Jake took Daniels reins again as they turned and followed a shallow draw up the slope to the west. As they entered a small stand of aspens, they heard the sound of a running horse on the trail from town.

Turning to Palliser Jake said, "You called that right."

Palliser nodded, then turned and looked back down the draw. The moon had climbed well above the eastern hills, and the rolling grassland below stood out stark and clear.

"That was a close thing," Jake continued. "How did you know?"

"Just a guess," Palliser answered. "I wondered why anyone would put out the light unless they maybe wanted to see out without bein' seen themselves. I shouldn't have told the world we were meetin' in the alley."

"Who do you think it was?" Jake asked.

"Most likely Carmody or Barry I'm guessin'. I seen that bald-faced chestnut Barry's been ridin' tied behind the saloon when I was waitin' for you."

Jake thought about that a moment. His mind was full of questions, but he knew they should get moving so in the end all he asked was, "What now?"

"I wish I knew this country better," Palliser said. "I suppose young Daniels knows his way around, but for the time bein' he's pretty much extra baggage."

Jake considered their options, then said, "For now why don't we ride parallel to the road, and when we hit one of them feeder creeks we'll follow it uphill. If we get to the source and we're still not in the cover of timber, we can water the horses and make a dry camp higher up."

"Sure. You lead the way."

"What are we doin' out here?" It was Daniels. Time and the cool night air were having their effect. Jake studied him a moment before speaking.

"Seems someone in Utica wants one or more of us dead," he said.

Daniels thought on this a moment, but his mind was sluggish. Then he looked at Jake and asked, "Did you really steal them horses?"

"No."

"How come Barry said you did?"

"Barry's a liar." The three men sat in silence as a warm breeze rising from the valley touched their faces.

"I figured as much." Daniels said. "I can handle my own horse from here." Without a word Jake handed him the reins, then turned and rode up out of the draw. Daniels, then Palliser fell in behind, the only sound the whisper of grass and the occasional hoof on stone.

—⁓—

Oliver Carmody stared out the back window of his office to the dark ridges against the night sky and swore. His loose cheeks and balding forehead, normally pale from a lack of sunlight, now were ghostly white in the moonlight. He had not bothered to relight the lamp, and in his preoccupation, was unaware of it. A fortune in gold waited almost within eyesight, almost within reach, and he was still unable to do a thing about it. He remembered the rainy summer night two years ago when Anson Cramer, the only patron in the saloon, had told him where it was. Cramer was a shiftless, down at the heels ner-do-well, so at first Carmody had been skeptical. For one thing, the geology was all wrong, and if the gold was indeed there, why hadn't Cramer done something about it? More for the sake of small talk than anything else, with half-hearted interest, Carmody had kept the conversation going. He'd asked Cramer how he knew the gold was there, and it was what came next that had sparked his interest.

"Jake Hoover showed me the spot when we was trailin' a herd o' elk," Cramer had slurred drunkenly. "He said there's plenty o' gold there alright. Trouble is you'd need water, and lots of it, to mine it. Only water available is a small spring way down the slope at the bottom of a dry wash. She's only a trickle and seasonal at best."

It was Jake Hoover's name that did it. Jake Hoover – a man with the uncanny ability to find gold – who seemed more interested in hunting and camping out in the wild country than in getting rich. Anson Cramer was a known associate of Hoover's and had accompanied him on several hunting trips when he was in the area. The geology did appear to be wrong, but Hoover was known for saying that gold is where you find it, and he was legendary for his ability to find it. The fact that he seemed more interested in finding it than having it was a puzzle to Carmody, but only made Cramer's story more believable.

Since that night Carmody had become a man obsessed. The more he'd learned about Hoover, the more he'd been convinced the gold was there. Doing some scouting around, he had realized there may be a solution to the lack of water. The barren, gravelly slopes where Hoover claimed the gold was located, were part of a hard scrabble outfit owned by a German immigrant, and they bordered land claimed by the Anchor D. About a half mile into the Anchor D holdings, and a few hundred yards further up the slope, was Tanner Springs, a sure and steady source of water that flowed year round. Only a slight rise in the shoulder of the hill prevented the water from tumbling down the dry wash, and with a little blasting, Carmody knew that could easily be remedied. He'd checked at the land office and found that Abe Daniels had filed on the springs, but because it was poor grazing land, Carmody figured there was a better than even chance he could be convinced to sell. He'd then purchased the land from the German immigrant, made a pretense at ranching, and then went to see Daniels with the story that he needed a better source of water for his venture to succeed. He made what he thought was a generous offer to purchase Tanner Springs, but Abe Daniels had flat out refused to sell. Carmody had left feeling angry, discouraged and unreasonably bitter toward Daniels. For a while he'd been at a loss for what to do, but then a chance conversation with Daniels' foreman had changed everything.

Barry harboured a deep resentment toward Nathan Daniels, who at the age of fourteen had come to live on the ranch after wearing out his welcome with Abe's sister in Denver. In the years that followed the resentment had grown to pure hatred, as Barry couldn't stand the thought of a shift-less fiddle-foot profiting from all his hard work and dedica-tion. As far as he was concerned, the Anchor D's success had been built on his back, so when he'd sensed the rift between Nathan and his father, he'd been only too willing to exploit it. Barry wanted the ranch, Carmody needed Tanner Springs, and Nathan was the weak link.

With considerable reservations, Carmody had let Barry in on his secret and promised him five percent of mine profits if he could help him swing the deal, and Barry was confi-dent he could do it. The plan was simple: put the Anchor D in a position where it was cash-strapped so that Carmody's offer to pay good money for marginal land would look like a convenient way out. If in the process the rift between the Daniels men could be widened, so much the better, as Barry knew Abe would be reluctant to leave the sum of his life's work to a son who would drink and gamble it away. Barry had talked Abe Daniels into borrowing money to purchase a herd of Hereford cattle, while making sure young Daniels had every opportunity to take advantage of the credit offered him at Carmody's tables. Once Nathan had accumulated what was deemed to be an unmanageable debt, Carmody would go to the elder Daniels and demand immediate payment. In the meantime, Barry had salted the Anchor D crew with rid-ers who were loyal to him rather than the brand; this loyalty being bought with the promise of a substantial payout once everything was settled. These riders made sure the Anchor D roundup was a failure, putting Abe under more pressure to accept Carmody's offer as a way of buying time.

The events in the saloon had caught both Carmody and Barry by surprise, and Carmody had realised immediately the threat Palliser's actions presented. Though he had never considered going as far as killing a man to get his gold, he had been quick to spur Barry on to, "do something to stop Palliser." What he didn't realize, was that when Barry had stepped out the back door to blaze away with his pistol, he'd been shooting at Daniels, not Palliser.

Barry had done some quick thinking of his own and realized that Daniels running off with a known horse thief, and an outlaw with his face on several reward dodgers, presented an unexpected opportunity. If young Daniels were "accidently" killed while making a getaway with known criminals, no one could blame the shooter, and the unfortunate incident would leave no one standing in the way of him one day owning the Anchor D. Now, as Barry was making the fast ride back to the ranch, it came to him that once the ranch was his he could double-cross Carmody and either demand a bigger cut, or freeze him out altogether. He made up his mind that he was going to do everything in his power to seize the opportunity. He was going to send Cob's crew on a manhunt to bring in Palliser and the horse thief, and to make sure Daniels never made it back to the ranch alive.

—◈—

"You call yourself Big Jake?" Palliser asked.

Across a small fire, whose warm light danced on their faces and touched the branches of the trees that hemmed them in, Jake was roused from pensive silence. "What's that?" he asked.

"Big Jake," Palliser repeated, a trace of a smile on his mouth. "That's what you called yourself before you slugged Adler."

A light of understanding came to Jake's eyes. "That was for killin' my horse," he said. "Big Jake was my horse."

"Big Jake is dead?" Daniels asked unbelievingly.

Jake nodded. "Adler shot him."

Daniels got to his feet, his young face troubled, then turned and walked off into the darkness. He'd been quiet but restless since learning of Barry and Carmody's collusion with regard to his drinking and gambling.

"I wish you wouldn't have slugged him." Palliser said.

"I reckon I had to," Jake said. "I did it for the wrong reason though."

"How's that?" Palliser asked.

Jake shrugged his shoulders, turned to look at Daniels who had come back to the fire, then said, "Big Jake's still dead. Sluggin' Adler didn't change that."

Palliser shook his head. "Well he had it comin'," he said. "I reckon it felt pretty good too."

Jake looked into the fire a moment before answering. Then he said reflectively, "I reckon we all got it comin' one way or another. Anyway, gettin' even never feels as good as you think it will, an' like I said, Jake's still dead. No, I needed to slug Adler alright, or we wouldn't have got out of there without someone gettin' killed. That ain't what I was thinkin' at the time though."

"I was gonna shoot him while I had the chance," Palliser said quietly. "That's why I was wishin' you never slugged him.

I couldn't very well do it with him out cold. There'll be hell to pay now for sure."

"Better that kind than the other kind I reckon," Jake said.

"What do you mean the other kind?" Palliser asked. Jake didn't answer right away, but just stared into the fire. With a sharp snap and pop, a pocket of pitch caught fire, sending a shower of sparks skyward while two coyotes yapped back and forth across the dark valley.

"What would Adler have done if it was you pinned behind the table?" Jake asked suddenly.

Palliser's head came up sharply. "He'd have bored me sure," he said, spitting out the words. "And enjoyed doin' it too!"

"Well, if you're sick of bein like him," Jake said thoughtfully, "I guess you made a good start tonight."

Daniels snorted loudly, and got back to his feet. "Honestly, Sullivan!" he said, "You're the craziest fella I ever met! I'm sure plannin' to kill somebody!"

Jake looked back to Daniels, and as he looked away he nodded and said, "I don't blame you for thinkin' it. Just so you know, if you go through with it there'll be a different kind of hell to pay. I killed a fella once a long time ago, and he had it comin' too I reckon. Trouble is, he had a wife an' kids, an' I ain't sure they had it comin'. Funny how it works though, 'cause I came close to doin' it again just to prove to myself I'd done right the first time. There's no tellin' where I'd have ended up if I hadn't met old Emilio."

"Who's Emilio?" Daniels asked.

"A Mexican fella I worked for. Best friend I ever had. I think he knew I was troubled by somethin', or maybe it woulda made no difference, but there was seldom a day went by he didn't start by sayin', 'What a mornin'! We can live today, Jake, for God's mercies are new every mornin'!"

Daniels shook his head. "Honestly," he said again, "I think that pistol whippin's addled your brains."

"No, he's right," Palliser said slowly. "I killed the second fella, and I never met Emilio."

For a time no one spoke. Daniels took his seat by the fire and sat brooding. A while later he shook his head in disgust. "I reckon Barry couldn't have done anything without me givin' him the raw material," he said.

"Why did he want to though, that's what I can't figure," Jake said. As if he hadn't heard him, Daniels continued down the same track.

"Here I figured I was kickin' Barry in the teeth while gettin' back at Dad." He shook his head and then was silent.

"Getting' back at your dad?" Jake asked.

Without taking his eyes from the fire Daniels said bitterly. "He never wanted me. I can understand him shippin' me off when I was a baby, but I kept waitin' for him to send for me an' he never did. He never did. Aunt Helen didn't want me either and she got tired of waitin' for dad, so she bought my ticket and sent me packin'. What a happy reunion that was."

Palliser got up and added a few sticks to the fire. "Well, Sullivan, if gun play is out, what's your plan?"

"I didn't say gun play was out," Jake said. "There might just be a better way."

Palliser straightened up. "I wish I could tell you more. Like I told you though, we was never told why, just what. There's gotta be more to it than just them cows up on the mesa and the jag they're holdin' over on Pine Creek though. That don't seem like a steal worth killin' over, and I don't see how it would involve Carmody. You sure you got no ideas?" Palliser looked across the fire at Daniels who shook his head.

"Dad never told me a thing about ranch business, and I never asked."

"What about Carmody? There's got to be a tie-in somewhere," Jake suggested.

Daniels thought a moment. "Carmody tried to buy Tanner Springs off Dad last fall, but Dad wouldn't sell."

"Tanner Springs?" Jake asked.

"They're way over to the southeast, next to some land Carmody owns. It's poor rangeland, but Dad didn't want to give up the water."

"Does Carmody run cows over there?" Palliser asked.

Daniels nodded. "He's got a small herd of culls, and he's makin' a half-hearted stab at ranchin'."

"Maybe he's found gold," Palliser said. Jake and Daniels turned to look at him. "You need water for more things than just waterin' stock," he continued. "Sometimes you need it for minin'. It's been my experience that when folks is willin' to kill over somethin', usually there's gold involved."

Jake looked thoughtfully into the fire. "That would explain a few things alright," he said.

"I know what we should do." It was Daniels. Jake and Palliser turned to him expectantly.

"We don't really know what's goin' on, but maybe that don't matter. We do know Barry's willin' to kill to keep them cows on the mesa a secret, so we know they do matter. I reckon if we was to drive them cows down to the ranch, his house of cards, whatever it is, would start tumblin' down. It's got to be so or he wouldn't a cared so much that Jake knew about 'em."

Jake and Palliser sat in silence for a moment, and then Palliser said emphatically, "That's it! Show up with them cows an' let things come apart all by themselves! It'll be easy. If me an' Daniels was to show up an' tell them boys Barry was ready to move the cows down to the ranch, they'd have no reason to think otherwise. Come to think of it, none of them boys up there's ever seen you, Jake, so the three of us could go. They'd just think you was one of the Anchor D riders."

"We'll have to make sure we get there before Barry does," Jake said. "They'll have no way of knowin' what happened in Utica tonight, and I doubt anyone will make it up there before tomorrow."

"Let's ride," Palliser said. "We should stick to the high-country to be on the safe side, so it'll be slow goin', but we can do it."

Jake kicked out the fire, and then followed the others to where their horses waited at the edge of the trees.

XIII

Abe Daniels lay awake well into the night, and when he finally fell asleep his dreams gave him no rest. He woke early, and with barely enough light to see by got dressed, tucked his crutch under his arm and hobbled out his bedroom door. It was dark at the foot of the stairway, but he looked up to where the light coming through the east window bathed the upstairs hallway with a soft and almost heavenly light. He stood still, while the clock on the mantle tick-tick-ticked and seemed to grow slowly louder. Tick-tick-tick-tick, Abe reached hesitantly for the banister, and then his hand rested there a moment before his grip tightened and he heaved himself up onto the first step.

Slowly, one labouring step at a time he climbed the stairs, and when he reached the top his heart was pounding, but it wasn't from exertion. He hesitated again, then with a determined set to his jaw, moved with an awkward jerky gait toward the lighted window at the end of the hall. The door to his right was closed, and though it took an effort of the will, now that he had forward motion he didn't allow himself to stop, but reached up and took a key from the ledge at the top of the door frame. His hand trembled as he inserted it in the lock, and when he gave it a turn, the metallic click was unnaturally loud in the stillness. Abe put a big hand on the doorknob, and then he stopped. His breathing was short and shallow, and his mouth was dry, and then he turned the knob and the door swung freely in. With his feet firmly planted in the hallway, Abe waited.

The room was dark and dead with a stale musty smell, and for a moment he was unsure. Then tucking his crutch up under his arm, Abe collected his courage and stepped inside. He didn't stop, but immediately crossed the floor, lifted the blind and let the light of the waking morning spill in through the window. Abe turned slowly and looked around. A film of dust covered everything and dead flies littered the floor, but he didn't see this. He saw a big double bed against the wall with its pretty bedspread with the yellow frills that reached the floor. At the head of the bed against the other wall was a little wooden cradle, painted yellow to match the bedspread. Here little Nathan had spent the first days of his life crying inconsolably for the mother who would never hold him. Abe walked slowly to it and put a rough hand on its smooth edge, then looked up to see a slimmer version of himself and beautiful Emma on their wedding day looking boldly out at the world from the safe confines of a small wooden picture frame. He resisted the urge to look away, but made himself study her face and was drawn to her eyes.

His memory filled in what the picture could not show, and he remembered how those eyes had been windows to a kind and gentle spirit, and how Emma always seemed to see the good things, even in him. Abe sighed, and it was a heavy sigh from the depth of his chest where his heart lived. He backed up a step, turned to sit carefully down on the edge of the bed and began to see the room. He saw the dust on the window ledge and the flyspecks on the wallpaper, the dead flies on the floor and the dirty window pane.

He dropped his gaze, shook his head and whispered, "God, I'm sorry. Emma… I'm so sorry," and then he wept. After a time he rose to his feet, crossed the floor to the closet and swung it open. He smelled the pungent odor of moth balls, and there were Emma's dresses hanging orderly and straight, and he knew the last person to touch them had been her. Reaching out, he hesitantly caressed the silky sleeve of the cream colored dress that had been her favorite and then dropped his hand to his side. Turning, he looked again at the picture above the cradle, and then he hobbled over, took it down and tucked it under his arm. When he left the room, he left the door open behind him. He crossed the hall to Nathan's room, stepped inside and laid the picture gently on the bed.

Nathan's knowledge of the country proved to be a great help, but it was the moonlight that made the difference. Though they'd been forced to take a roundabout route, they made the ridge north of Two Canyons well before there was light in the eastern sky. With both horses and riders played out, they'd made a dry camp with the mesa rising dark and ominous a mile in the distance. They had no food or blankets, and there was little conversation as each man sought out a piece of dry ground beneath the pines. Jake, still weakened from his ordeal, slept hard, deep and dreamless, and Nathan, who was the first up and moving, had to rouse him.

"Mornin', Sullivan," he said. "I think we best get ridin'."

Jake sat up, nodded and put on his hat.

"I saddled your horse," Nathan said. "I figured you could use the sleep."

Jake looked at Daniels, his eyes showing mild surprise, and then nodded. "Thanks," he said. He sat there a moment, his tongue thick and his mouth dry, a persistent pounding in his head, then got stiffly to his feet. They mounted up in silence, and Palliser took the lead.

Winding through the trees, they followed the ridge till they reached the timbered slopes below the mesa. Presently they came to what looked like a game trail, and Palliser drew rein. After briefly studying the ground he said, "If Barry came up from the ranch he'd most likely take this trail. No one's been up here since them last showers so we're on time I reckon."

"How many men are with the cattle?" Daniels asked.

"As far as I know, just two."

"Maybe one of us should hang back a bit just in case," Jake said.

Palliser thought a moment then nodded. "That's probably a good idea," he said. "We should be alright for a bit though. It don't open up till after the bog."

Jake nodded and when Palliser turned his horse up the hill they moved out in single file. The climb was gradual but steady, and here and there other trails intersected theirs, so that soon it was worn wide and deep. They were riding through a thick stand of tall, slender pines when Palliser reined in and dismounted. Jake, who was bringing up the rear, looked past Daniels to see a crude rail fence winding up and away through the trees. Palliser untied two rails that served as a gate, drug them off to the side, and then mounted up.

"We may as well leave it open I reckon," he said. "There's another gate further south, but we'll bring them cows this way." Neither Jake nor Daniels responded, but Daniels was clearly interested in what he was witnessing. Once through the gate, the terrain levelled off and the pines gave way to thick, stunted spruce. Cattle sign was everywhere, and the trail wound through ground that was soft, wet and hummocky. Soon there was water showing between clumps of coarse grass, and the horses had to fight through mud that came half-way to their hocks. They were just gaining solid ground when Jake spotted a Hereford cow and calf before they spun away to disappear amongst the thinning spruce. Palliser turned his horse to face Jake.

"We're almost there," he said. "Maybe find a place where you can keep watch from the edge of the trees."

Jake nodded, and then watched as Palliser and Daniels followed a bend in the trail and were gone from sight behind a thick stand of stunted evergreens. Turning, he saw a gap in the spruce to his left, so he took it, and wound his way between dark, heavy boughs till he came abruptly to the clearing. He drew up short, careful to stay under cover. Spread out before him was a, grassy meadow that was about half a mile across at its widest point, rising gradually to the foot of a boulder-strewn slope about a half mile in the distance. The tops of evergreens showed above the ridge, and at the base of the hill stood a small log cabin and a set of corrals. About fifty cow-calf pairs were spread across the clearing, and they had their heads up, eyeing Palliser and Daniels, who were riding slowly across the meadow. Jake looked back to the cabin, noting that there was smoke rising from the chimney, and then the door swung open and a man stepped out to watch Palliser and Nathan's approach. Even at this distance Jake could see he cradled a rifle in his arm.

———✦———

Lee-two closed the oven door, and then straightened to wipe her forehead with the back of her hand. It was warm in the kitchen, and she'd taken off her father's coat, which was heavier than the one she'd lost. She couldn't be sure, but she didn't think Nathan or Jake had returned from town, and she was worried and pre-occupied. She'd heard a lone horse come in late last night, but could only guess what it meant, and she was anxious to see what information she could glean from the crew's morning conversation. She looked over at her father, who was cutting thick slices from a large ham, then turned to reach for a canister of sugar on a shelf high above her head. She was just setting it down when she heard the sound of the outside door coming open. Turning, she was startled to see the bulky form of Abe Daniels lumbering in through the door. She turned back quickly, and then threw a glance to where her father's coat hung from the back of a chair at the far end of the table.

"Mr. Daniel, good mohning," her father said.

"Mornin', Lee. Got any coffee?"

"Coffee not boyo. Soon, soon."

Abe Daniels slacked into the chair closest to the door as Lee-one walked around the end of the table. He picked up his coat and took it to Lee-two, who still hadn't turned around.

"Please. Moa wood owside. Make coffee boyo."

Lee-two smiled gratefully at her father, shrugged into the coat, then turned around. Abe Daniels was watching her closely, and she smiled hesitantly, and then looked down at the floor as she walked past him.

"Lee-two."

She stopped short in the doorway, her heart beating rapidly, and then turned to faced Abe Daniels.

"Please, sit down."

Lee-two glanced nervously at her father, whose movements had frozen, his knife poised over the ham. Looking back to Daniels without speaking, she took a chair at the end of the table.

"I had a visitor last night," Daniels said. "A fella they claim tried to steal some of my horses." Daniels was watching Lee-two closely, and she was unable to hide the startled look in her eyes. "A Mr. Jake Sullivan," he continued. "Is he a friend of yours?"

Lee-two glanced again at her father, and then nodded hesitantly.

"It's pretty warm in here," Daniels said not unkindly. "It's pretty warm outside too for that matter. There's no need for you to wear the coat." Lee-two's eyes betrayed her alarm, but Daniels continued. "It's alright. I can't believe I didn't know sooner. Sullivan told me a few things and I figured if this was true some of the other stuff might be true also. I want you to start wearin' a dress from now on. If any one of my crew don't treat you like a lady I'll send him packin' an' that's a promise. Will you do that?" Lee-two's eyes inexplicably filled with tears, and Daniels asked clumsily, "What's wrong?"

"I am sorry," Lee-two said, wiping at the tears. "I do not know why I am crying."

Abe put an awkward hand on her arm, and then asked, "Will you start wearin' your dress then?"

Lee-two shook her head and sniffed. "I do not have one," she said meekly.

Abe sat back in his chair, looked down at the table for a moment, then back to Lee-two. He drew in a deep breath and let it out slowly. After a long pause he said, "I wonder if I could ask a favor of you."

Lee-two looked at him with eyes still moist and waited.

"There's a room up at my house could use a thorough cleanin'," Abe continued. "I'm not up to it. Could you do that for me?"

Lee-two nodded. "Of course, Mr. Daniels," she said.

"There's some dresses in the closet there that should be close to the right size. Pick out three or four that you like an' you can have 'em. Make sure you take at least one that's for dressin' up pretty."

Lee-two's eyes showed both surprise and humble disbelief. "Thank you, Mr. Daniels," she said softly. "You are very kind."

An awkward silence followed and for a while no one spoke. Then Lee-one said, "Coffee boyo. I get foe you."

As Lee-one walked around the table to the stove, Abe noted the hitch in his gate and felt a sudden unexpected kinship with the Lees. He also felt a touch of self-derision at the pity he'd heaped upon himself as an excuse not to work through his own handicap. As Lee-one poured the coffee, Abe turned to Lee-two and asked suddenly, "What do you think of my son? What do you think of Nathan? Please, be honest. Don't lie to me because I'm his father."

Lee-two looked into Abe's eyes, and hers were straightforward and genuine. "Nathan is troubled and sometimes foolish, but my father and I like him very much."

"Why?"

"Nathan is kind and respectful, even to a Chinese man who limps and to his son who is not very strong. Nathan gave us this job when we had nothing. My father and I are very grateful."

Abe sat quiet – deep in thought with his coffee forgotten. When he looked again at Lee-two he asked, "Who are you afraid of?"

At that moment they heard the front door of the cook-house come open, and the fleeting look that crossed Lee-two's eyes was the answer to Abe's question.

"Lee!" Cliff Barry bellowed. There were quick hard foot-steps on the floor and then Barry stepped into the kitchen. "Lee!" he said again, before he was brought up short seeing Abe Daniels seated at the table. "Abe! What are you doin' here?" he asked.

Abe studied Barry a moment and he wondered. Then he asked, "What's the hurry, Barry?"

Barry hesitated before answering, his eyes cold and calcu-lating. "It won't be news you'll want to hear."

Abe straightened in his chair. "Let's hear it," he said.

Standing feet apart with his thumbs in his pockets Barry nodded grimly, then said, "I rode into town yesterday evening and was there just long enough to find out your boy rode off with the horse thief and a fella who's wanted for stickin' up a bank in Wyoming. The horse thief slugged one of my men, and there was some shootin' in the alley behind Carmody's before they went ridin' hell for leather out of town. They was headin' this way I'm told, so I'm organisin' a man hunt."

Though Barry's words startled Abe, his gaze never faltered as he studied his foreman, trying to see the man in a different light and wondering if it was necessary. He remembered the horse thief saying something about Nathan being in trouble and not knowing it, and curiously now, the words had the ring of truth. He waited, trying to process the information, and his silence seemed to make Barry uncomfortable. As Abe watched, the man shifted his weight nervously, and his eyes darted over to Lee, then back to him. Finally, Abe changed the subject and asked, "Who's around?"

The question clearly caught Barry off guard, but then he answered crisply, "Cob's here with some of the boys that was on the south gather."

"Who might they be?"

"Hanson, Orrin, Taylor, and Hatfield."

Abe thought he detected a hint of wariness in his foreman's eyes and he asked, "Who are Taylor and Orrin?"

Barry straightened up, and a defensive edge crept into his voice. "A couple of new riders I took on to help with the roundup."

"Who did the horse thief slug?" Abe asked.

Barry hesitated. "Chance Adler."

"Another new hand?"

Barry nodded.

"One of Cob's crew?"

Again Barry nodded. Abe studied Barry a moment, and again Barry shifted his feet uncomfortably under his gaze.

"Maybe the reason Arnie's crew had a better gather," Abe said quietly, "was because he had most of the riders that know the country. How come you split them up that way?"

Barry's eyes grew hard, and he couldn't conceal his anger. He swallowed then said, "I picked most of the new boys up from over south so I figured they'd know some of that country. I guess in hindsight I shoulda done things different, but I spent a good deal of time with Cob's crew, and we rode that country hard."

Daniels nodded. "I'm sure you did," he said. "You can call off your manhunt though. Nathan's bound to turn up on his own, and as far as the other two go, I ain't interested. I got my horses back and we're a long way from Wyomin'. Leave the manhuntin' to the law if they think it's worth their while. You got Anchor D business to attend to. I want you to take your crew down to the basin and spell off Arnie. Tell him to hurry back here with some riders so they can give that south country a goin' over only men that know the high country can give it. Who knows, maybe they'll turn up enough of them steers so I can meet my payment."

It was plain Barry didn't like being told how to do his job, and the hard arrogance he wore out of habit was difficult to fight down, but he answered meekly enough. "You're right, Abe. I was loosin' sight of priorities. I reckon it galls me a little that you think Arnie'll do a better job than I done though."

Abe didn't let up any. "You didn't turn up a lot of cattle. Maybe Arnie will. Time'll tell I suppose."

Barry nodded, and then glaring at Lee-one said, "We'll want to eat before we ride, so make it quick." He turned on his heel, and moments later they heard the front door slam.

Abe took a drink of his coffee before heaving himself to his feet. Leaning heavily on the table he looked at Lee-two and said, "When you're finished feedin' those boys come on up to the house. I'd sure appreciate help with that room, and I want you to have a look at them dresses."

"Thank you, Mr. Daniels."

Abe picked up his crutch, and as he turned to leave Lee-two said hesitantly, "Mr. Daniels?"

Abe turned back to face her.

"I don't want to speak out of place, but there is something I think you should know."

"What is it?"

Lee-two bit her lip and looked questioningly at her father. When she looked back to Abe she said, "Mr. Barry sometimes talks very freely, as he thinks I cannot speak English."

Abe Daniels looked expectantly at Lee-two, and she continued.

"Yesterday Mr. Barry told this man, Chance Adler, to make sure he got Nathan drunk. He also told him it may be necessary to kill him."

A look of anger, mixed with shock and disbelief flared up in Abe's eyes, but somehow he knew Lee-two spoke the truth. Sitting back down he said quietly, "Tell me everything you know."

XIV

Cliff Barry paused briefly on the cookhouse porch, his eyes dark and his jaw clenched. He was in big trouble and he knew it. No doubt Palliser had told young Daniels about his part in the horse stealing frame up, and if Abe found out about it all hope was lost. There was no way around it, Nathan Daniels had to die. With him out of the way the other two would be out of it. No one would believe their story, and because they knew this they would drift. Stepping down onto the hard packed compound, a desperate plan began to take shape in his mind. He wasn't going himself to relieve the basin roundup crew, at least not right away. He'd send three of his riders and keep Orrin and Taylor back. They were a couple of hard cases and would do what they were told with no questions asked. What Abe had said was most likely true. Nathan would drift in on his own, and because he had no idea his life was in danger, he'd have no reason for caution. His death could be blamed on a "falling out among thieves", and they could leave his body where it fell, only to be discovered later. With any luck they'd get it over with quickly, and he could join the basin round up crew without anyone being the wiser.

Barry was tired, as he'd had a long sleepless night. He'd posted himself just off the trail a couple of miles from the ranch gate in hopes of intercepting Daniels. When no one had shown up, he'd grown impatient and ridden back towards town. At first light he'd come upon the place where the three riders had left the trail to climb the ridge to the west, and immediately he'd headed back to the Anchor D. There were only two logical approaches to the ranch coming off that ridge, so Barry figured their odds were good. He'd have Cob stop in Utica and tell Adler what to do if Daniels showed up there. If Adler were to pick a fight with Nathan after what had transpired last night, no one would blame him. The crew was just finishing saddling up when Barry got to the barn.

"Head up to the cookhouse boys. Breakfast will be ready shortly. Cob, I need to have a word with you."

The mesa top behind the cabin was a long chain of small clearings, and even in the trees, there was grazing for the cattle. Jake had seen two springs besides the one at the bog, and though the grass was chewed down the cattle were in good shape. There was still the intermittent bawling of cows frantically searching for their calves, but the milling herd was beginning to move out more willingly. Palliser had the two riders from the cabin take the point, as they knew the best trail down, and though they hadn't discussed it, Jake reasoned this was also a preventative measure in case they rode into an ambush. He watched as Palliser cut back an errant steer, then they both fell in behind as the last of the cattle splashed across the bog to break into a trot on the downhill into the pines.

Jake glanced at Palliser. "I think we might just pull this off," he said.

"Here's hopin'," Palliser replied, but his face was grim.

—⁓—

Cliff Barry led a tight and silent little cavalcade out the front gate of the Anchor D. Just over the first rise and out of sight of the buildings he reined in, turned and faced the others.

"Any questions?" he asked, and was met with silence. "Alright. We should be joinin' you boys shortly. Don't be in any big hurry to send Arnie's crew back here." Cob nodded, then turned toward town and two of the riders fell in behind him. Barry watched their backs for a moment, and then turned to look at Taylor and Orrin. "Don't miss," he said, then jerked his horse savagely around to ride away without a backward glance.

He rode past the draw where he'd waited most of the night, hesitated, then moved on. He'd left plenty of tracks and didn't think it wise to shoot Daniels from the same ambush, as he wanted nothing that pointed to him. Riding parallel to the road, but about a hundred yards on the uphill side, he came to a second draw. The bottom was choked with willows, and further up the hill it took a sharp bend to the right. Just over the shoulder of the hill he could see the tops of an aspen stand. He turned his horse uphill, then tied him out of sight among the trees and drew his rifle from its scabbard. Turning, he made his way back down the draw on foot.

He had a hard time finding the perfect place to watch from, and second guessed himself several times before settling on what he thought was the best spot. Resting his rifle in the crotch of a willow, he sighted down the barrel and gave a grunt of satisfaction, then settled down to wait.

The waiting was the hardest part. The sun was warm on his shoulders, and with no sleep the night before, he was soon struggling to keep his eyes open. He broke off a short piece of a willow branch, popped it in his mouth and began aggressively chewing on it, moving it back and forth from one cheek to the other. Presently the drowsiness left him, and he thought he was okay.

Barry's eyes came open to the sound of hooves on the road and the rattle of steel wheels. A buggy with two outriders was coming toward him, and they'd already passed the spot where he could have gotten off a good shot without having to move his rifle, and there were now willow branches blocking his vision. He felt suddenly vulnerable, and realized that once the buggy had passed by, he'd no longer be under cover. He'd been so focused on Daniels coming up the road, that he'd failed to consider what he'd do if someone else showed up. Leaving his rifle in the crotch of the tree for fear the movement might attract attention, he slowly lowered himself down into the grass. With his chest pressed against the ground, he peered around the edge of a grassy hummock and hoped for the best. The first rider to come into view was Sheriff Kingman, and as the buggy came into his line of sight, Barry almost lifted his head in surprise. It was Carmody! The second outrider was Adler! Barry didn't dare move, but his mind was racing. *What was going on? What was Carmody doing with Kingman? Why was Carmody heading for the Anchor D before the trap was set?* Barry waited till the buggy was out of sight around a bend in the road, and then sat up. He was desperate to know what was going on, but knew he couldn't afford to leave his post. If he showed up at the ranch, Abe Daniels would wonder why, and they'd know he was in the area instead of with Cob, whose lie was to give him an alibi. He began to curse violently, and then his suspicious mind grabbed hold of one terrible thought.

"Carmody's double crossin' me," he said out loud. "He's figured out a way to cut me outa the loop."

A bleak and dark mood settled on Barry, and though he knew he couldn't be sure, he couldn't shake the nagging doubts. The worst of it was, there was nothing he could do about it, and he'd have to just let things happen and hope he could pick up the pieces later. He yanked his rifle from the tree, and stormed around till he found a spot where he'd have better cover if anyone came up behind him.

Abe Daniels was sitting at the kitchen table when he heard Lee-two's footsteps coming down the stairs, and moments later she walked into the room. Instinctively he rose to his feet as she stopped to stand self-consciously before him. She was wearing one of Emma's work dresses, dark blue and plain, and it fit her perfectly. A mix of emotions fought for his heart as Lee-two looked down and almost reverently smoothed the skirts with her hands, but when she looked hesitantly back up at him, the feeling that this was somehow deeply right won out.

"You look beautiful, Lee-two," he said.

She looked quickly down at the dress again, then back to Abe. "You are too kind, Mr. Daniels," she said. "And I would be most grateful to accept this one dress. The room told me many stories, and I understand that this is a very expensive gift."

Abe looked quickly away as tears threatened to well up in his eyes. Looking back to Lee-two he motioned awkwardly to an empty chair and said, "Please, sit down. Can I pour you a cup of coffee?"

Lee-two looked over at the stove, then back to Daniels. "No, Mr. Daniels," she said, "you sit down. I will get some coffee for you."

Abe shook his head. "Please, Lee-two. It's been too long since there's been a lady in this house."

He motioned to the chair again, and Lee-two hesitated before sitting gracefully down. It was hard for her to watch as Abe struggled with his crutch, and only able to use one hand, had to make several trips to bring two cups, a sugar bowl and the coffee pot to the table.

As he poured her coffee he said apologetically, "Sorry, but I got no cream."

Lee-two looked up at him and her smile touched his heart. "Mr. Daniels," she said. "You are making me feel like a princess."

Abe laughed, and it was deep and unexpected, and he felt suddenly clean and new as he took a seat. "That's good," he said. "That's good. You make me feel like a gentleman."

Lee-two smiled as she put a spoonful of sugar in her coffee. They shared a comfortable silence, and then Abe spoke.

"Lee-two," he said. "I want you to have them dresses. All of them." Lee-two made as if to protest, but Abe lifted a big hand to cut her off. "Please. You'd be doin' me a favor. I've made a shrine out of Emma's things long enough. I'd have done a sight better lookin' out for her son... our son. I didn't know how to lose a wife, and I think I lost a son in the process."

"It is not too late, Mr. Daniels. It is not too late for you and Nathan."

Abe looked at Lee-two with eyes earnest and pleading. "I don't know how to start," he said.

Lee-two placed a reassuring hand on his forearm. "One of you has to say I'm sorry first," she said.

—◊◊◊—

The cattle were thirsty by the time they reached the Two Canyons cabin. Barry's two riders had already crossed the river and they turned to watch from the rise while the cattle milled and pushed, spreading out upstream along the bank. The occasional bawling from the cows and calves intensified as Palliser reined in beside Jake.

"I think maybe we're gonna be okay," he said. "I figured if Barry got wise and was gonna try to stop us it'd be here at the crossing."

Jake nodded as he turned to watch the cattle. "It's a narrow part of the trail that's for sure." His bay's head came up, and Jake followed its line of sight to see Chickadee standing at the rail gate watching them. He glanced again at the cattle, realized it would be awhile before they'd all had a drink, turned to Palliser and said, "We may as well give 'em time to mother up." When Palliser nodded, Jake turned his horse and rode over to the barn, dismounted and threw his reins over the hitch rail. Stepping inside, he grabbed a halter and then walked across the yard to where the black filly waited. He climbed the rail fence, slipped the halter on her head, and then led her out through the gate and back to his gelding. Mounting up, he rode over to where Palliser waited. Palliser looked at the filly and eyed Jake questioningly. When no explanation was forthcoming, he turned back to watch Daniels, who had begun pushing the cattle across the river. Leading Chickadee, Jake moved down the slope to help out, and soon they were across the ford and on the trail to the Anchor D.

The cattle were trail-broke now and they made good time. As the trees on the uphill side began to thin out, Jake looked ahead and saw the tall, grassy, pyramid-like hill topped with ragged boulders, and remembered it as the landmark where they'd hit the main valley and swing back northeast toward the ranch. *Only three miles to go*, he thought.

A small group of steers broke away and dropped down to the river. Daniels slid his horse down the bank, let them take on water, and then moved them out. Instead of climbing the slope back up to the other cattle, the steers followed the river, and when they broke clear of the trees, Nathan was right behind them.

CRACK!

The sharp report of a rifle split the still, warm air, and Nathan was driven backward in the saddle. Instantly the cattle ahead began to mill as Daniels, hunched forward and off balance, fought his horse around and away from the shooter. Three more shots hammered out in rapid succession as his buckskin lunged wild and reckless into the herd. A white-faced cow just behind him went to her knees bawling pitifully, and then the cattle were stampeding in all directions. Jake let go of the filly's lead shank, and with his gelding moving at a dead run, weaved through the crazed and scattered herd toward Daniels. Behind him he heard Palliser's rifle making a hard statement over the sound of the guns below, and when he broke free of the cattle, Jake had to veer sharply to the right to avoid Nathan's buckskin, which was in a blind run-away. One rein had broken off just below the bit and the other was flapping wildly. Jake kneed his horse alongside, and with hooves pounding, leaned over and got hold of the loose rein. He managed to slow the horse down as it made a wide circle around him, and then he led him up into the shelter of a small aspen bluff. He barely had time to glance at Nathan's strained face and bloody torso before Palliser was upon them.

"Quick! Get him up to them boulders!" he yelled.

Jake heard the sound of a running horse, and glancing over his shoulder, saw a rider on the ridge across the river. It was one of the men who'd helped bring down the cattle, and he was riding hard to cut them off from behind. The other shooters were trapped on the far side of the herd, and for the time being were out of good shooting range. Jake glanced back to Palliser and nodded, and with bullets singing past their ears and whining off the rocks, they broke from the trees in a driving run, charging up the open hillside. Jake was in the lead, while Palliser, keeping himself between Nathan and the riflemen, rode beside Daniels, keeping his sagging frame upright in the saddle. They made the shelter of the boulders and Jake bailed off his gelding, barely in time to catch Daniels who was coming off the near side as his horse shied away from its burden. Palliser paid them no mind as he made a flying dismount, and then scrambled to the edge of the boulders to send three fast shots down the slope.

Nathan's face was pale and twisted, and he looked up at Jake with eyes flushed and hot.

"How are you doin' there, young fella?" Jake asked as he glanced down at Nathan's bloody shirt front.

"I'm breathin'," Nathan responded hoarsely. "It's startin' to hurt like the blazes though."

The wound was high and on the right side, and though it was bleeding freely, Jake was hopeful the bullet had missed the lung. He glanced around, and realized they couldn't have picked a better place to make a stand as the boulders offered cover in all directions, and their attackers had no choice but to cross an open hillside if they wanted to close in.

"Let's see what we can do about that wound," Jake said, looking back to Nathan. Nathan nodded, and Jake undid his buttons as a volley of shots sounded from below. Palliser's rifle was loud in response and then there was silence. The bullet hole was dark and oozing, and it was lower down than Jake had hoped. He tried not to let the concern show in his face as he said, "Hold your hand over it, okay, Nathan?" Nathan nodded meekly, and Jake quickly took off his own shirt. He tore a strip off the bottom, wadded it up and handed it to Nathan. "Press that tight against it. I'm gonna have a look at your back."

Jake found no exit wound, but just below the shoulder blade and near the outside edge of Nathan's back, he could see a dark ugly lump under bruised and stretched skin. Palliser was at his side and his face was grim.

Jake looked at him questioningly. "Should we cut it out?" he asked.

Palliser shook his head. "I don't know. If we can get him to a doctor it would be better for him to do it. It's gotta come out for sure, but if we do it now it's sure gonna bleed."

Jake nodded. "I'll ride," he said.

"I think that's best anyway," Palliser agreed. "I should be able to hold 'em off for a while, and he's gonna need help."

"How are you fixed for bullets?" Jake asked as he slipped back into his shirt.

"Not near enough. I'll have to be careful not to waste too many. You better get goin' right away before they think of it. The sooner you get back here with help an' more shells the better chance we got."

"What about him?" Jake asked, motioning toward Daniels. "I better tie that bandage in place."

"Forget it," Palliser said. "I can handle it. Get your horse while I make a quick circle around the perimeter. When you hear me sendin' shot's down the hill, you make your break on the back side."

Jake nodded, and drew the pistol from his waistband. "Here," he said. "This might make the difference." He began shucking shells from the cylinder, and then continued, "Nathan's got some in his shell belt too."

"Hold on," Palliser protested. "You might need them bullets yourself."

"I'll keep a couple," Jake said. "Luck to ya."

"Same to you." Palliser said, glancing quickly at Nathan. Then crouching low, he disappeared among the rocks on the western rim.

Jake mounted up, and leaning forward over the saddle horn, picked his way through the boulders toward the eastern slope of the hill. He had just reached the outer edge when Palliser's rifle hammered out behind him, and without taking time to scout out the best way down, he urged his bay over the edge, taking the steep grade in a reckless sliding run. Almost out of control and gaining speed with each lengthening stride, he reached the bottom, and came abruptly upon a wide wash cut deep by the recent rains. With rocks clattering over the rim, he reined hard to the left, the jarring, jolting turn sending fresh stabbing pain through his injured ribs. With clenched teeth and a firm set to his jaw, he followed the wash for a few yards, and then found a sharp cut in the bank that took him to the bottom. Pausing just a moment, he reassured his horse with a pat on the neck, and then moved out at a brisk trot down a narrow gorge.

He'd traveled only thirty yards, when the ground began to slope sharply down and away. He was slowing the bay in preparation for what would be a steep descent, when the head and shoulders of a man appeared directly in front of him. The man had his head down and was labouring for breath, making the climb on foot, and Jake recognized him as one of the riders who'd jumped him at the Two Canyons cabin. He heard Jake a split second later, and as his heat-flushed face came up in surprise, Jake put the spurs to his startled gelding. The horse shot forward as the man threw his rifle to his shoulder, and though Jake's intent was to run him over, his gelding swerved instinctively at the last moment. Jake lifted a foot as he blew past, and his boot and part of his stirrup caught the man square in the face, the force of the impact twisting Jake sideways in the saddle. He didn't have the luxury to look back and assess the damage, as his horse was now in a free falling run down an impossibly steep grade. Jake felt the cantle slamming into his lower back as he strained to lean backward, his right arm stretched out behind him. The horse hit the valley floor, his chest and head driven toward the ground as he fought to keep his feet, and then he was up and running, stretching out in long, even strides, eating up the ground in beautiful flowing motion as Jake turned him in a wide circle toward home.

Movement off to his left caught his attention, and turning, Jake saw a horse and rider coming up out of the creek bed. The man was riding hard to cut him off, and had the angle on him. Jake drew his pistol as the distance closed, and as he saw the oncoming rider bring his gun down in a chopping motion, he triggered off two fast shots of his own. He had no idea if he'd scored a hit, but the man's horse planted his front feet and went to pitching. Jake's gelding pinned back his ears with a desperate burst of speed and then they were by and running free.

Jake shoved his pistol back in his waistband and let the horse have his head. He glanced over his shoulder, and when he saw no pursuit, he slowed the horse to a lope, then a long extended trot. He kept the pace up for a couple of minutes, and was about to move back into a gallop when he was startled by the sound of hooves on the trail behind him. Instantly he urged the bay into a run, but when he threw a look back, he was relieved to see Chickadee coming hard in an attempt to catch them. Jake slowed up, and when the filly pulled alongside, he reached out and took hold of her lead shank. Though she was obviously worked up and frightened, she didn't fight it, but took comfort in the companionship. Then they were off again, moving in tandem with the halter shank hanging loose between them.

XV

A be Daniels sat on the porch and packed his pipe with thick, strong fingers. Lee-two was just mounting the steps to the cookhouse, still wearing the blue dress and packing a precious bundle under her arm. Abe smiled and shook his head. "The boys are sure in for one big surprise," he said out loud. Striking a match, he lit his pipe, took a good pull, and as he exhaled, looked around the ranch yard. He felt a strange mix of forgotten pride in the place, and a sense of remorse over wasted time. Remembering Lee-two's open and humble gratitude for the dresses he'd given her, he smiled again. Emma would have approved. A sure, strong peace settled on him, and it was welcome beyond belief.

Abe's head came up sharply at the sound of approaching horses. As he watched, a buggy and two riders came through the front gate and pulled up in front of the barn. Instead of waiting for them to come to him, Abe heaved himself to his feet, picked up his crutch, and took the porch stairs one slow step at a time.

The riders had dismounted, and the driver of the buggy was stepping down when the nearest man turned and saw Abe approaching. Leading his horse, he strode purposefully up the slope toward him. It was Sheriff Kingman.

"Howdy, Sheriff," Abe said, as he eyed the tall, stoop-shouldered man who stopped to stand before him. "Is this business or a social call?"

Kingman regarded Abe for a moment, and his clean shaven face was pleasant, though a trace of concern showed in his eyes. "Howdy yourself, Abe," he said. "It's nice to see you up and around."

Abe nodded. "About time I reckon. What can I do for you?" Abe looked past Kingman to the pair at the barn. "I see you brought an entourage."

Kingman glanced over his shoulder then back to Abe. "They're not with me," he said. "We just met up at the edge of town and were goin' the same way so we rode together."

"Who is it?"

"Carmody and one of your boys."

"Carmody? What's he after?"

Kingman shrugged his shoulders. "Didn't say, and I didn't ask," he said. "Anyway, about your first question, I ain't sure if it's business or social. Maybe a little bit of both."

Abe looked at him questioningly and Kingman continued.

"Nathan got in a bit of a ruckus at Carmody's last night after him and another one of your boys rode in to report the stolen horses."

"Did he break any laws?" Abe asked, remembering Barry's story.

"Not that I know of. There was some shootin' in the alley out back of the saloon, but I don't know what it was about, and near as I can tell there was no harm done."

"You figure that's what Carmody's here for?"

"Like I said, I don't know," Kingman responded. "I wanted to talk to you about the horse thief though. Seems the fella with Carmody's one of the boys that rode him down and caught him with the goods."

Abe's eyebrows came up. "Oh," he said. "What's his name?"

"Adler. Chance Adler." A knowing light came into Abe's eyes as Kingman continued. "He was part of that ruckus too. I'm still tryin' to piece it all together, and I was hopin' maybe you could help me. Seems the horse thief showed up and slugged this fella before headin' out of town with your boy and the rider who reported the stolen horses. It sure don't make no sense to me."

Abe nodded. "Maybe we should go talk to Adler," he said.

"Sure," Kingman responded. "He ain't been much of a help so far." Kingman turned and fell in beside Abe, purposefully shortening his stride. As they approached the barn, both Carmody and Adler turned to face them. Daniels was shocked at the appearance of Adler's face, which was a sickly mixture of purple, blue and yellow around bloodshot eyes, and he was sure the swollen and flattened nose must be broken.

Daniels glance shifted to Carmody, who greeted him with a nod and said, "Hello, Daniels. Good to see you up and around."

Daniels grunted his acknowledgment, remembering Kingman's similar greeting, then he turned to Adler and asked bluntly, "Who are you?"

Adler lifted his head, clearly taken aback, then said carefully, "Chance Adler."

"What are you doin' here?"

Adler shifted his feet uncomfortably. "I work here," he said.

"Doin' what?"

"Whatever Barry tells me to do," Adler replied, his pride bringing an edge of fight into his voice.

Abe watched him a moment, then asked, "What's the last thing he told you to do?"

Adler's eyes shifted nervously to Kingman, then back to Daniels, and he said, "He told me to ride into Utica to report the stolen horses and to give the sheriff a description of the horse thief."

Abe turned to Kingman and asked, "Is this the fella that told you someone stole my horses?"

Kingman shook his head. "No," he said. "It was another fella, a Dan Palliser. Him and your boy came into my office yesterday. Like I said, Palliser's the fella that rode out with your boy and the horse thief. Adler here came into my office early this mornin' and told me to check my reward dodgers. He said he figured he recognised Palliser from a wanted poster in Wyoming. I checked my dodgers and sure enough, I found a Dan Palliser who's wanted both in Wyoming and Utah."

Abe was silent and thoughtful a moment before lifting his gaze to Adler with eyes cold and hard. Then he turned and addressed Kingman saying, "Sheriff, I sure don't know what's goin' on, but don't it strike you as odd that the fella Palliser accused of stealing my horses willingly rides out of town with him a few hours later? Don't it strike you as odd that Adler here remembered them dodgers after Sullivan slugged him?" Turning back to Adler he asked, "How long were you ridin' with this Palliser fella? Wasn't he with you when you caught up with the horse thief?"

"He was there." Adler said.

Abe shook his head. "Sheriff Kingman," he said. "Let me clear one thing up. No one stole any of my horses, and anyone who says different is a liar. I've never even laid eyes on this fella with the purple face before, and he sure enough don't work for me." Turning to Carmody he asked, "Does he work for you?"

Carmody was quick to respond. "No. No, he doesn't work for me."

"Why was you travelin' together?"

"We just met up on the road, that's all."

Adler's eyes settled on Carmody, and his look was thick and arrogant, but he said nothing. Then he looked back to Daniels who was speaking to him.

"Well, Mr. Adler, if you don't work for Carmody and you don't work for me, state your business then ride on out of here. I see no reason for you to stick around."

Adler watched Daniels for a moment with eyes that smoldered. He glanced from Kingman to Carmody, then back to Daniels, shook his head and said, "I reckon you're right. I got no reason to stick around." He stepped into the saddle, turned and rode from the yard without a backward glance.

"Abe, what's goin' on?" Kingman asked, but Daniels ignored him. Instead he turned to Carmody.

"Sorry to keep you waiting, Carmody. What can I do for you?"

Carmody was on unsure footing. Abe Daniels had a fire in his eyes that he hadn't seen before, and as much as he hated to admit it, he was indebted to Adler. He'd been the one to tell Adler to go see the sheriff about Palliser, for though he had nothing to do with the assembling of Barry's riders, he knew something about them. Had Adler chosen to implicate him, he'd have found himself in an uncomfortable position. He had all of Nathan's gambling notes with him, signed by his hand, but he didn't want to play his trump card at the wrong time. Last night he'd come to the decision not to wait for Barry's go-ahead, as the defection of Palliser had put their plans on shaky ground. Now after witnessing the exchange between Daniels and Adler, he was convinced Barry was losing his power to influence the situation. He was on his own as far as he could see, and he'd have to make sure to keep a comfortable distance between himself and Barry. He didn't think there was any way Barry could give away his part in things without putting himself in a bad light, but he couldn't be sure. Trying his best to sound unconcerned, he looked at Daniels and said, "It can wait, Abe. Looks like you got a lot on your plate right now, and this ain't that important."

"Nonsense," Abe said. "You didn't drive all the way out here just to turn around and go back. What's on your mind?"

Before Carmody had the chance to answer, the sound of pounding hooves caught their attention, and all three turned to see a big man on a blood bay horse come charging through the south gate. He was leading a black horse, and both it and his bay were glistening with sweat. The rider came to a hard stop directly in front of them and all eyes went from the horses to the man. Of the three, only Daniels had met Jake Sullivan, and that had been in the dark of night where he'd been unable to get a good look at him. Barry had been the one watching through a crack in the door when Sullivan had taken Nathan out of the saloon, so Carmody had never seen the man. Both he and Daniels knew instinctively who he was however, as Jake's hot eyes went from one to the other, then settled on Daniels. Jake's iron jaw was beard stubbled, and his shirt was dirty and torn with the un-tucked hem hanging ragged above his belt line. The butt of a pistol showed against a lean hard stomach and dried blood covered his hands. A commanding presence held the men on the ground silent, as the big bay horse tossed its head, pushing on the bit and prancing impatiently.

"Daniels!" Jake's voice was sharp and urgent. "We need help quick! We were bringin' in some cows from up on the mesa when Barry's men ambushed us. Nathan's caught a bad one and we got to get him to a doctor. Palliser's tryin' to hold them off but we ain't got much time!"

"Nathan's been shot?" Abe exclaimed.

Jake nodded; his face grim.

"But Barry and his men just rode out for the basin!" Abe protested. Turning to Carmody he continued, "You must have met them on your way out here!"

Carmody was quick to see the need to distance himself from Barry as much as possible. He felt a sense of panic rising in his chest as he realized Barry had gone further than he'd ever dreamed of, and there was the very real danger he'd be sucked in with him. Now was as good a time as any to try and keep that from happening. He shook his head quickly and said, "We only met three riders on the way out here. Barry wasn't with them."

"God help us!" Daniels pleaded, his voice heavy with passion. Turning back to Jake he asked, "Where are they? How far back up the trail?"

"They hit us right where the Two Canyons trail hits the main valley," Jake responded. "We got Nathan up in them boulders at the top of that steep hill, but I don't know how long Palliser can hold them off."

"How bad is Nathan? Can he ride?"

Jake shook his head. "We'll need a wagon," he said.

Abe's eyes grew dark as he put his hands on his hips, shook his head and said through clenched teeth, "And we ain't got one here."

"I can take my buggy." Carmody cut in. "If you can find me a rifle I'd be more than willing to come along."

"Thanks, Carmody," Abe said, "We could use you that's for sure."

Kingman spoke up. "We better ride," he said. "Where do you keep your rifles?"

"There's a gun rack in the den just to the right of the door. I've been using it for a bedroom. Maybe pull the sheets off the bed and we can use them for bandages. I'll climb in with Carmody and get started. You boy's will have no trouble catching us."

"We'll need some shells too," Jake said.

Abe nodded. "You'll find 'em there. Let's get a move on!"

Abe climbed up into the buggy with Carmody, who slapped the lines to the horses. As the buggy lurched into motion and clattered away toward the south gate, Jake turned to face Sheriff Kingman.

"You mind fetchin' them rifles, Sheriff?" he asked. "I gotta turn this filly loose in the horse pasture." Without a word Kingman nodded and stepped into the saddle.

Carmody and Daniels had made less than a mile when Jake and Sheriff Kingman caught up with them. Carmody reined in the team, and as Kingman handed over the rifles and the bed sheet, Abe glanced at Jake, and then at the horse he was riding.

"That's one of them colts, ain't it?" he said. When Jake nodded, he continued. "Fine lookin' animal. Nathan's the one that located them horses."

Again Jake nodded. "He's got a good eye for horseflesh, I reckon."

Daniels turned his head quickly away, looked up the trail, and then savagely worked the lever on his Winchester. As he let the hammer off cock, he said grimly, "Let's get movin'."

Carmody put the buggy in motion, and Jake and Kingman rode ahead, fanning out on each side of the trail. They travelled in silence and soon began to come upon small groups of cattle scattered along the valley floor. Glancing back at Daniels, Jake knew that regardless of what happened from here on in, Barry's time at the Anchor D was over. There was no sound of gunfire ahead, and he felt the tension mounting, fearing they might be too late. As the steep boulder-topped hill came into view, the only thing that could be heard was the persistent bawling of a calf, and the intermittent bellowing of a cow. Jake glanced anxiously up the slope, and as they rounded the shoulder of the hill, they saw a lone cow grazing beside the body of her trampled calf. A little ways off, a calf nuzzled the cold udder of its dead mother. Jake scanned the hillside, and then half hidden in the grass at the foot of the hill, he saw the body of a man twisted awkwardly in death. With a sense of apprehension Jake pulled his horse to a stop, and then movement high among the rocks caught his attention. It was Palliser. He stepped into view and urged Jake forward with a frantic wave of his arm. Quickly, Jake glanced over at Abe who was already reaching behind him for the bed sheet. He sidestepped the bay over to the buggy, took the sheet from Abe's extended hand, then turned and took the slope in a hard, driving run. As he crested the hill, the urgency in Palliser's face told him Nathan was still alive. He dismounted, hearing the hooves of Kingman's horse pounding the hill behind him. Without a word he followed Palliser into the boulders.

Nathan lay on his side, his back against a large smooth stone, his wounded side to the ground. His face was gray and his breathing short and shallow, but he was conscious. Jake knelt down beside him, and then turned to look at Palliser.

"Wouldn't it hurt less if he was layin' on his good side?" he asked.

Palliser shook his head. "I didn't want his good lung fillin' up. I rode with a fella that was an army doctor in the war, an' he said that's how you should do it."

Jake nodded and looked back to Nathan. "Your pa's just down the hill with a buggy," he said. "We're gonna have to get you down there so we can get you to a doctor." Nathan nodded weakly and Jake turned to see Kingman dismount beside Palliser. "Sheriff, could you bring our horses down. I think it'll take both me an' Dan to move Nathan."

"Sure," Kingman responded.

Jake stood and handed the sheriff his reins, then looking at the bed sheet asked, "You think we should just wrap this tight around him right over his shirt?"

Palliser bit his lip, thought a moment then said, "I think that's best. Otherwise he'll likely start bleedin' again."

Jake helped Nathan to a sitting position, and then held him upright while Palliser knelt down and carefully began wrapping the bed sheet around his ribs.

"You made good time, Sullivan," Palliser said glancing up at Jake. "They broke off the attack almost immediately after you left."

"I see you nailed one of 'em," Jake said.

Palliser nodded, his face sober. "That happened just as you were leavin'."

Jake moved to get behind Nathan and then slipped an arm under each shoulder. Palliser took hold of his legs at the knees, and they lifted him gently off the ground. Nathan made no sound, but by the way he clenched his teeth, Jake could tell they were hurting him. When they reached the edge of the boulders, they set him back down so Palliser could get a better grip. He turned around so he wouldn't need to walk backwards, wrapped an arm around each leg, and then they started down the hill. Kingman was already at the buggy, and as Jake watched, he and Abe walked over to where the dead outlaw lay. While Abe held his horse, Kingman heaved the man's body up and over his saddle. By the time Jake and Palliser got Nathan to the buggy, they were back with their grisly burden tied in place. As Jake and Palliser lifted Nathan onto the buggy floor, Abe hobbled over to stand beside them. He placed a firm hand on Nathan's shoulder, and Nathan turned to regard him, his face strained and pale.

"Hang on, Nathan, we'll get you to the doctor as quick as possible," Abe said.

Nathan nodded, and Abe spoke again. "Nathan," he said thickly. "I'm sorry."

Nathan waited a moment, his eyes on his father, then he said weakly, "I'm sorry too, Dad. We got some talkin' to do."

Abe nodded. "We'll do it too, son." Turning to Jake he said, "Could you ride for town and fetch the doctor? We'll get Nathan down to the house."

Jake nodded and Palliser said, "I'm comin' with you."

The two men mounted up and took the trail home at a hard gallop. As the sound of hoof beats faded in the distance, Abe climbed into the back of the buggy to sit beside Nathan and help hold him upright. Carmody slowly turned the team around, and his mind was in turmoil. He'd never dreamed Barry would go so far, and it was inevitable that his part in things would be found out. He would be hard pressed to prove he hadn't been in on all of it. He decided then that, gold or no gold, he had no choice but to come clean. Looking over his shoulder he cleared his throat.

"Abe," he said. Abe turned to look at him, and after a brief silence Carmody continued. "There's some things I need to tell you."

XVI

Cliff Barry couldn't remember feeling so alone and pow-erless. He had no idea what was going on, and it seemed less and less likely that his attempt to ambush Nathan Daniels was going to succeed. He'd been tempted to come out of hid-ing when Adler had ridden by on his way back to town, but then had decided to stick it out. Now as the afternoon wore on he grew more anxious and restless, and finally, could take it no longer. With one last look down the trail in both direc-tions, he shook his head, swore in frustration and got to his feet. He climbed the hill to where his horse waited, mounted up and headed for Utica. He would hunt up Adler and see what information he could glean from him. Carmody would soon be heading back too, and Barry found himself looking forward to meeting with him. If Carmody had double-crossed him, he'd soon find himself wishing he hadn't.

—◊—

Lee-two hung her dish towel on the handle of the oven door, and then took a seat at the table. Her father was in the house, and in a way she wished he wasn't. She'd made up her mind that she wanted to be wearing the beautiful cream-colored dress the next time she saw Jake, and she thought her father might not approve. She knew he was afraid her hopes would be dashed and her heart would be broken, and she was a little afraid of it too. Now that she was wearing a woman's clothes, she was more aware of her short hair, and she desperately wanted to be beautiful. She wondered what her father would say if she changed dresses, and she knew that if he told her not too, she could not disobey. Maybe it was being deceitful, but she decided to wait untill he was out of the house before going ahead with it. Her thoughts returned to Jake. She had been in the house when he'd ridden into the yard earlier, but her father had seen him. He'd told her how Mr. Daniels had gotten into a buggy with another man, and that Jake and another rider had followed them. He told her they had both been carrying rifles, and remembering this, she whispered a prayer for the hundredth time that afternoon. Because she found it hard not to be anxious when she wasn't busy, she got back to her feet, stepped out the door and headed for the house. Her heart jumped at the sound of hoof beats, and then it leapt when she saw Jake and another man riding toward the front gate on horses glistening with sweat. They were moving at a fast trot, and neither of them so much as glanced her way. She felt a sense of relief knowing Jake was alright, but even so, her heart was heavy as she turned for the house. She decided then that putting on the cream-colored dress was a stupid idea.

—◊—

"What do ya mean you quit?" Barry asked, unable to keep the pent up frustration from his voice. He was sitting across the table from Adler in the Cosmopolitan Saloon, a tired and dingy place at the north end of town not far from the stables.

Adler shrugged his shoulders and took another drink of his beer. "It's over, Barry," he said, setting his mug back down on the table. "I can read the writin' on the wall even if you can't."

"You're scared of Palliser and Sullivan," Barry accused, hoping to goad Adler.

Adler looked across the table, a bored expression in his eyes. "Anyway," he said, "you owe me some money and I'm wonderin' how you're gonna pay up."

"But you never finished the job!" Barry protested. "And what do you mean, 'How am I gonna pay up?'" Adler didn't answer right away, but leaned back in his chair, picking at his teeth with a thumbnail. The smug look on the man's face infuriated Barry, though he knew better than to let his feelings show.

Adler straightened up. "I may not have finished the job," he said, "but I'm finished just the same. Old man Daniels gave me my walkin' papers. I figure you're on thin ice too, so that's why I want to get paid off while you still got a say. Without the Anchor D behind you, you're just a broke saddlebum same as me."

Barry felt a mix of cautious fear and cold anger, but he kept his voice level. "What makes you think I'm on thin ice?" he asked.

Again Adler shrugged. "Just a feelin' I guess. Old man Daniels had a fire in his eyes, an' he'll be callin' the shots from here on in I figure. Also, you got to remember, if it ever comes to a showdown, over half the crew's gonna back him. I ain't buckin' them odds."

"What makes you think it'll come to a showdown?" Barry asked.

"Just a feelin'."

Barry sat silently, staring blankly through the open doors of the saloon. Adler's cryptic words bothered him more than he cared to admit, and he fought down a rising sense of panic. Turning back to Adler he said, "Wait here. I'll get your money. I'm only payin' you for a month though."

Adler grinned at him, and Barry didn't like the odd light in his eyes. "You'll pay me for the full two months," he said. "Besides, what difference does it make? It's Daniels who's payin' me, not you."

Barry glared across the table at Adler, who returned his stare. It was Barry who looked away, and then he sighed and got to his feet. "Wait here," he said. "I'll be right back."

Barry stepped out onto the boardwalk, paused a moment, then turned to walk toward the bank. Two riders were coming down the street toward him, and suddenly he was brought up short. Stopping in mid-stride, he shrank quickly back into a doorway. The riders were Jake Sullivan and Dan Palliser, and it was clear their horses had been ridden hard. Half a block away, they turned and disappeared up a side street, and after hesitating briefly, Barry stepped back out onto the boardwalk. He walked to the corner and then carefully stepped down onto the street to have a look. Sullivan and Palliser's horses were tied in front of the doctor's office three buildings down, and as Barry hurried to cross the street, his mind was racing. Maybe he'd put some lead into Nathan after all! If they were hunting up the doctor it must mean that he was still alive, but hit pretty hard! That was it of course. No wonder Nathan hadn't returned to the ranch and his ambush had failed. Nathan was unable to ride!

What to do now though, that was the question. Barry stopped and considered turning around and telling Adler. No, he was out of it. He'd pay him off and be done with it. The fewer people who knew what he was up to the better. He would follow Sullivan and Palliser back to their camp and finish what he'd started. Because Sullivan was wanted for horse stealing, there was no way they would have taken Nathan back to the ranch, so they had to be hiding out somewhere. Their boldness surprised him though, but then he reasoned they may figure no one in Utica was likely to recognize them as neither of them had spent much time around town. Barry stopped in mid-stride again. What if Palliser had told Nathan the truth about the horse theft, and Nathan had managed to make it back to tell his father? Barry realized suddenly that this was a very real possibility, and his only hope was that Taylor and Orrin would have intercepted them had they tried to make the ranch. He moved out again, and as he entered the bank he decided that once he'd withdrawn Adler's money, he'd stop by and see if Carmody had made it back. What he needed more than anything right now was information, and Carmody offered him the best chance of getting some.

Barry left the bank and took a side street to the alley. He walked the block and a half to Carmody's, mounted the back steps and tried the door. It was locked. He cursed under his breath, turned and sat down on the step. He wondered if he should wait for Carmody's return, as it might be foolhardy to blunder on without knowing what had happened. On the other hand, if he waited too long he might miss the opportunity to follow Sullivan and Palliser. He decided he'd go pay Adler off, then find a place where he could sit and watch the street in case either Carmody arrived, or Sullivan and Palliser left. He got to his feet and made his way back to the Cosmopolitan. Stepping into the dimly lit room, he crossed the floor, and without taking a seat threw Adler's money on the table.

"Two months' worth," he said, "Thanks for quittin' just before things come to a head."

Adler rose lazily to his feet, took the money and pocketed it. "Things already came to a head, Barry," he said. "You're just too thick-headed to see it."

Barry glared again at Adler, who watched him from behind his swollen nose, daring him to make an issue of it and enjoying the satisfaction of knowing he wouldn't. A moment later Barry turned on his heel and left without saying another word.

He'd only gone a few steps when movement up the street brought him to a stop a second time. Sheriff Kingman was riding toward him, and everyone on the street had turned to watch. Kingman was leading a horse, and draped over the horse's saddle was the body of a man. Barry stood frozen where he was, watching as the sheriff dismounted in front of his office halfway up the next block. When Kingman had tied his horses and disappeared inside, Barry moved quickly forward on wooden legs, blanketed by a sick feeling of apprehension. A crowd of curious onlookers was gathering around the dead man, but Barry only needed to throw a quick glance his way as he walked by to know that it was Taylor. He knew instantly as well that Adler had been right. Things had come to a head, and he'd been too thick-headed to see it. He'd only gone a couple of steps when he heard someone behind him say, "One of Cliff Barry's men," and he picked up his pace without looking back.

—⁓—

Doctor John Callaghen took his fleet-footed saddle horse to the Anchor D instead of driving his buggy. A veteran of the frontier, where time and distance were often the difference between life and death, he'd long since had a saddle maker build him a special set of saddlebags that could carry the essential tools of his trade. Because Jake and Palliser's horses were pretty much spent, they'd stayed behind to give them a chance to rest up and cool down before making the ride back to the ranch. After off saddling, they'd headed for the restaurant at the hotel, a convenient short walk from the barn.

The evening shadows were lengthening, and the sun would soon be lost behind the Little Belt Mountains when they stepped back onto the boardwalk. The first thing they noticed was the crowd in front of the Sheriff's Office a couple of blocks up the street, and Palliser turned to Jake.

"Looks like Kingman made it back."

Jake nodded. "Looks that way," he agreed. "I wonder how Nathan made the trip down to the ranch."

"Let's head up that way and see what news we can get," Palliser said.

Jake, however, was reluctant to deal with the crowd and the inevitable questions from people hungry for information on things that didn't concern them. After a brief pause he said, "You go ahead, Dan. I think I'll saddle up, and then head over to Lehman's Merchandise. I got a couple of purchases to make."

Palliser turned to face Jake. "Maybe I should come with you," he said.

Jake regarded Palliser a moment before speaking. "Are you ridin' herd on me, Dan?" he asked.

Palliser shifted his feet uncomfortably, looked to the gathering crowd on the street, then back to Jake. "I reckon you might say that," he said. When Jake didn't respond he continued. "Barry's still around someplace, and so is Adler. This here ain't over, Jake, and meanin' no disrespect, I think you might be in a little over your head where Adler's concerned."

Jake nodded, his face serious. "No disrespect taken," he said. "I'll be careful, and thanks." Palliser didn't say anything, but Jake could tell he still had something on his mind. "What is it?" he prompted.

Palliser was obviously uncomfortable, but then he responded. "I don't quite know how to say this right, Jake, and it might come out soundin' a little foolish, but you met you're Emilio, and I reckon I finally met mine. It feels good bein' on the right side of things for a change, and with all that's gone on before, I don't know if folks will let me stay there. I reckon I'm in over my head as far as Adler's concerned too, but for some reason I don't really care. This would maybe be a good time to die."

Jake watched Palliser, and for a while the two men stood in silence. Then Jake said, "You head on up to the Sheriff's Office. I'll go saddle Dan, do my shoppin', and then meet you back at the barn."

"You'll saddle Dan?" Palliser asked, surprise in his voice.

Jake nodded. "I just decided that would be a good name for that bay. Everyone had him pegged for an outlaw 'cause they didn't know any better. See you in a bit." Jake turned toward the barn and Palliser stopped him.

"Jake," he said. Jake stopped in midstride and turned to face him. "Just don't let Adler choose the time and place." Jake nodded and turned to go. Palliser watched his back for a moment, and then reluctantly headed for the Sheriff's Office.

From across the street, Adler stood in the darkened doorway of the Cosmopolitan Saloon and watched as Sullivan and Palliser went their separate ways. It hit him then, that he had unfinished business to attend to before he rode out of town. Barry's comment about him being afraid of Palliser and the horse thief had not been far from the mark. There was something not right about a man who would jump another while outnumbered and covered by more than one gun. The horse thief was a big stubborn man, and he'd seen men like him take a lot of lead and keep shooting, dead on their feet but too stubborn to quit. He, along with Palliser, was no bargain by any means. Now they'd split up, but still Adler wanted to be sure. He remembered the shotgun Carmody kept in his room behind the saloon and smiled. Turning on his heel, he left by the back door and took the alley to Carmody's.

Cliff Barry was scared. He'd gone directly back to the bank to get a road stake, but had found it closed. He remembered Adler's comment about him being just another broke saddle bum, and it brought on a different kind of fear. It occurred to him then that Adler would soon be leaving town, and he would be carrying the $200 he'd just paid him. This then would be his road stake. He was glad for the rifle in his saddle scabbard, though the irony that only this afternoon he'd been willing to kill for a gold mine, and now was planning to do the same for two months' worth of a gunman's wages, escaped him completely. He realized, though, that even if he didn't get out of town before Adler, Adler wouldn't travel far before finding a place to camp for the night, and this might provide as good an opportunity for an ambush as any. He decided then to wait till it got darker and things quieted down on the street before picking up his gelding at the stables.

He needed to find somewhere to keep out of sight until then, and chose for his place of hiding the outhouse behind the bank. He'd waited in the close, urine stained air for a long half hour, when the sound of a buggy travelling the alley outside caught his attention. Standing, he peered through a small moon-shaped window in the door, and was surprised to see Carmody driving by. Barry sat back down, wondering what he should do. His good sense told him to wait right where he was, but curiosity, and the need to know what had gone on at the Anchor D were too strong, and with a heavy sigh, he got to his feet and stepped cautiously into the alley. No one was around, and it occurred to him that this might be as good a time as any to make a break for it. Most of the activity in town would be centered around the drinking establishments and the Sheriff's Office. He moved quickly down the alley toward Carmody's, and when he got there, he stepped around the buggy, surprised to see the back door smashed to splinters and sagging on its hinges. He mounted the stairs, and Carmody turned around quickly at his entrance.

"Are you the one who kicked in my door?" Carmody demanded angrily.

Barry shook his head, then asked menacingly, "What was you doin' out at the Anchor D?"

Carmody straightened up, paused a moment, then said truthfully. "I went out to see if I could close the deal. I figured Palliser's jumpin' ship put our plans in jeopardy."

"What did Daniels have to say?"

"We never got around to discussing it. Sullivan came ridin' in with news of your ambush, and we all made a mad dash to go help. What were you thinkin'?!"

Barry ignored the question and asked, "Who's we?"

"What?" Carmody asked, not following Barry's line of thought.

"Who's we?" he asked again persistently. "Who went ridin' out to help?"

Carmody paused, and then said, "Me, Abe, Sullivan and Sheriff Kingman. You're in big trouble, Barry. Kingman's puttin' out a warrant for your arrest."

"What for?"

"Attempted murder and cattle rustling."

"I wasn't there," Barry said flatly. Then he added, "Who got shot?"

"Nathan Daniels." Carmody said, and here he stretched the truth. "He's hit pretty hard and I don't expect he'll make the night. That charge will be upgraded to murder."

"Like I said, I wasn't there."

"You're gonna have a hard time provin' it. Where were you? You got an alibi?"

Barry didn't bother answering, and he knew his situation was hopeless. Then an ugly expression came into his eyes and he looked at Carmody accusingly. "Why did you go with 'em to help out?" he asked.

Carmody glared right back and said, "What else could I do. Stick my neck in the noose along with yours? I never had anything to do with your foolhardy plans!"

Barry drew his pistol, cocked it and pointed it point blank at Carmody's face. "You wouldn't be double crossin' me now would you?" he asked.

Carmody looked past the pistol unflinching. "For what? After today we got nothin'. Funny thing though. All of a sudden this business of mine and my life the way it is started lookin' pretty good next to the alternative."

"Alternative?" Barry asked.

"Just what you're lookin' at, Barry," Carmody said quietly. "A long drop at the end of a short rope. Was I you, I'd be thinkin' about how you're gonna get out of here. You let that pistol off and you ain't got a chance." Here Carmody was guessing, but he added, "Kingman's got your horse spotted, so when you go to get him, he'll have you."

Barry stared down his pistol at Carmody for a long moment, and then he said, "Just so you ain't helpin' him."

"Now why would I do that?" Carmody asked.

Barry watched him with eyes that smoldered, then let his pistol off cock, jammed it back into his holster, and turned and fled through the broken door. He paused in the alley, fighting down the panic that was a tight knot in his chest and throat. What Carmody had said was true of course. Kingman would be watching his horse, so he'd have to steal one. Then, like a frightened alley cat, Barry began slinking from building to building, working his way toward the barn at the north end of town.

On the opposite side of the street, Jake was about to leave the store when he remembered Palliser's words, 'Don't let Adler chose the time and place'. Turning around, he strode across the floor and left by a side door, then made his way to the alley out back. He'd saddled his horse and left him tied in front of the stables, and reasoned it was perhaps wise to approach him from a different direction. He paused behind the store, taking the time to change into his new shirt and to strap on his new holster. The wide shiny yellow ribbon he left in the bag. He was about to resume his walk down the alley when he was brought up short. There, tied between a storage shed and an outhouse, almost out of sight, was Adler's roman-nosed paint! With his heart pounding, Jake put a hand on the butt of his pistol and looked cautiously around. There seemed to be no one in the alley, but still he waited, shrinking back into the deeper shadows behind the buildings. A dog barked at the edge of town, and somewhere in the distance he could hear children laughing, then all was quiet.

As he waited it came to him that this could be his opportunity to choose the time and place, and after a brief hesitation, he took a quick look around, and then crossed the yard to where Adler's horse waited.

"Easy there, fella," Jake said as the horse's head came up at his approach. "Easy now." Jake glanced over his shoulder, then threw the stirrup up over the saddle and loosened the cinch. He glanced back behind the cantle and noticed that Adler had his bedroll tied in place, so he knew he was planning on leaving. He noticed something else too. Adler had a set of hobbles hanging beside the billet strap, and immediately another thought came to him. Unfastening the hobbles, he stooped and put them around the horse's front legs just below the fetlock joint, so they would be hidden in the grass and weeds. As he worked he couldn't help but feel that his exposed back was wide open and vulnerable, and he fumbled with the buckle in his haste. He was just straightening up when the heavy blast of a shotgun ripped into the evening, and his heart jumped in his chest. Adler's horse stood calm and unconcerned as Jake hurried back to the shelter of the buildings.

Chance Adler was confident as he waited between the barn and the feed store. From where he stood, he could only see the hip of the horse thief's big bay, but he was dead sure that when Sullivan came to mount up, he would be able to step out into the clear for a point blank shot. It came so quickly it almost took him by surprise. The horse backed up a step and Adler could see part of the horse thief's shoulder and the brim of his hat. Thumbing back the hammers on the shotgun, he stepped into the open. To his dismay, he had to squint as he was looking directly into the setting sun, but then as the dark silhouette before him found the saddle, he threw the gun to his shoulder and let go with both barrels. So confident was he of his shot, that he didn't allow himself the luxury of surveying his handy work, but immediately turned and fled down the dark narrow space between the buildings. As he broke free into the alley, he could hear wild shouting on the street.

Jake only had seconds to wait before he heard the sound of running feet, and as Adler came into view, his hand dropped to take the pistol from his holster. He could feel the tension mounting as Adler reached his horse and ducked around behind to slam the shotgun into the scabbard. Quickly and efficiently then, Adler came back around, jerked his reins free and stepped into the saddle. As the stirrup took his weight, the loosened saddle spun around, throwing Adler well off to the side. A grunt of shock and surprise escaped him as he reached frantically with his free hand to take a fistful of mane in an effort to keep from falling. As the startled horse lunged forward, Jake was moving, and when the gelding's front feet hit the ground his hobbled legs buckled. Fighting to gain his feet, the horse's violent lurching motion brought the saddle completely over, and Adler lost his grip and was driven shoulders first into the ground. Jake had closed the distance, and when Adler's startled face came up, he was looking right into the barrel of Jake's gun only inches away. The shock of recognition was like a physical blow, and seeing the man he'd just killed looking at him from behind the pistol was too much. With an animal-like shriek of fear and desperation, instinct took over and Adler's hand streaked for his gun, which was still held firmly in place by the leather thong over the hammer. As his hand closed on the pistol grip, Jake stepped in quickly to bring the barrel of his gun down hard and heavy across the side of the Adler's head. Adler crumpled like a lifeless ragdoll to the ground, and Jake stood over him, feet apart and breathing heavily. Behind him, Adler's gelding had quit fighting, but stood pounding a back foot into the ground in protest of the saddle hanging under his belly. Jake ignored the horse; his eye's fixed on Adler's limp form at his feet. Holstering his pistol, he stooped to relieve Adler of his. He looked at the gun a moment, then jammed it behind his belt, reached down and took hold of Adler's collar. He then unceremoniously dragged the outlaw down the alley, around the store and to the street.

Main Street was alive with frantic activity, but the first thing Jake saw was Dan Palliser standing in the middle of the road beside his bay gelding. Palliser turned at his approach, a look of pure relief washing across his face.

"What have you got there?" he asked.

"A murderer, I'm guessin'," Jake said. He let go of his burden at Palliser's feet, breathing hard from the exertion.

Palliser nodded as he looked down at Adler. "Is he dead?" he asked, a complete lack of concern in his voice.

Jake shook his head no. "Just pistol whipped," he said. "I caught him comin' up the alley just after the shotgun blast. He was carryin' a shotgun too."

Palliser looked at Jake. "He's the one killed Barry then I reckon. Near about cut him in half. Barry was gettin' on your horse when he shot him, so I reckon he was gunnin' for you."

Jake's brow wrinkled in surprise. "Barry's dead?" he asked.

Palliser nodded, and after a pause, shook his head and said with deep feeling. "When I seen your horse come runnin' up the street with the stirrups flappin, and right after I heard the shotgun too, well I sure feared the worst. Looks like you didn't need me ridin' herd on you after all."

Jake turned as Sheriff Kingman and another man approached, and then looked back to Palliser. "That ain't the case at all, Dan," he said. "It was because you told me not to let Adler pick the time and place that it all worked out. Now if only Nathan can pull through, this here mess will all be over."

Palliser turned to Kingman who had stopped beside him and was looking down at Adler. "Here's your killer, Sheriff," Palliser said.

Kingman looked from him to Jake, and Jake said, "Dan can explain everythin' to you if you don't mind, Sheriff. I left a package in the alley out back, and I better go deal with Adler's horse."

Kingman nodded, his expression serious, and Jake turned and left.

—⟶⟶—

Lee-one looked up as his daughter stepped out of the bed-room. She'd changed back into the blue work dress, and he wished she hadn't. He said nothing, but he could see she'd been crying, and his heart went out to her. He knew there was nothing he could do, and he almost told her that she was beautiful no matter what she wore, but he knew these were words she needed to hear from someone else. Instead he got to his feet and said, "I'm going to step outside for a while."

Lee-two looked at him and smiled politely. "Okay, father. I will be going to bed soon I think."

Lee-one paused at the door, turned back and said, "I love you, little bird."

"Thank you, father."

"I am sure Mr. Sullivan will be back soon." Lee-two looked down at the floor, and her father continued. "It is good that Nathan is doing well. It is something to thank God for."

Lee-two looked at him and smiled. "We have much to be thankful for," she said.

Lee-one waited a moment, and then stepped out into the darkness. He limped around to the front of the cookhouse, stepped up onto the porch and took a seat on a stump chair. The night was still and starry, and the frogs were keeping up a steady chorus. Across the compound a lantern had been hung above the barn door, and it made a warm circle of light reaching out across the ground and up toward the eaves. Looking up toward the big house, he saw there were still several lights burning, and he felt strangely lonely. After a time he got back to his feet, paused a moment, and then turned for home. He was almost to the front door when he heard tired hoof beats in the darkness. Turning, he saw the dim form of two riders gradually come to clarity as they neared the barn. He saw now that there were three horses, and that one had an empty saddle. He held his breath subconsciously, and then let it out in relief as he saw the rider on the far side was Jake Sullivan. He considered walking down to him, but then thought better of it. The men dismounted in front of the barn, and he saw Jake look his way, and he wondered if the light from their house was showing him up. As he watched, Jake handed his reins to the other man, then turned and walked toward him. Lee-one was unsure what to do, so he waited where he was, summoning his courage. When Jake stopped before him, Lee-one could feel his weariness, though he could tell he had something on his mind.

Jake nodded and said, "Evenin', Mr. Lee." Glancing over Lee-one's shoulder to the lighted window of the small house, he continued, "Glad to see you're still up."

Lee-one nodded politely, then said maybe a bit too abruptly, "Mr. Sulliwan. I muss speak to you." Jake waited, and then Lee-one continued. "I not good englis, but dis impoetant. I muss speak you abow my daughta. My daughta…"

"Lee-one," Jake interrupted. Lee-one quit speaking and for a moment both men stood in silence. Jake sighed deeply, shook his head and then continued earnestly. "I know you love your daughter, and bein' I'm the wrong race and all, I'm sure you had somethin' better in mind for her. But I love her too, and if she'll have me and if you'll give me time, I aim to prove to the both of you that I'm good enough for her, though I guess I know I ain't and never will be. I'm a stubborn man, Mr. Lee, and if you take Lee-two back to China I aim to go with you. As long as I think there's a hope she could ever love me I'll be stickin' around. If I find out she don't though and never will, I'll leave her alone an' be miserable for the rest of my life."

Lee-one stood silent a moment, then looked at Jake and said, "Dis sound wery interesting, Mr. Sulliwan. You will need talk to Lee-two. I tink she still awake."

Jake shifted his feet anxiously, and then said, "Tell her not to go to bed. I'll be right back. I got to get something for her." His weariness forgotten, Jake turned and ran back toward the barn.

Ten minutes later he stood in front of the Lee's door. He drew a deep breath, let it out, and then knocked. He heard quick, light footsteps on the other side and his heart beat rapidly. The door swung open and Lee-two stood before him, framed in the doorway with the light behind her. She was wearing a rich, cream-colored dress that reached in full folds to the floor. The sleeves were short and fitted, revealing strong, slender arms, and the dipping neckline was a soft complement to the slightly darker skin of her neck and the base of her throat. She said nothing, waiting for Jake to speak, but whatever words he'd planned to say were lost to him. Finally he said, "Lee-two, you're beautiful!"

Lee-two smiled graciously, "Would you please come in, Mr. Sullivan. Father has gone to bed, but I just put some coffee on."

"Thanks, Lee-two," Jake said. "Coffee sounds great, but could you step outside first? I got somethin' I want to show you."

Lee-two looked at him curiously and then nodded. "Of course, Mr. Sullivan." Stepping outside, she closed the door behind her. Jake took her elbow and guided her around to the front of the cookshack. There, tied to the hitching rail was Chickadee, and she had a bright yellow ribbon tied in a bow around her neck.

"She's yours, Lee-two," Jake said. "Or at least she will be. I'm gonna buy her from Abe; then it'll be official."

"It is Chickadee!" Lee-two exclaimed, "Oh, Jake, I do not know what to say!"

Jake shifted his weight nervously, and then said, "It might seem like a strange gift, Lee-two, but I knew you liked her, and I figured if you had a horse you might want to learn to ride. To be honest, I was lookin' for an excuse to drop in on you from time to time, and I figured maybe I could give you ridin' lessons."

Lee-two turned to face Jake, and she took a tentative step closer. "Jake," she said. "The kitchen window was open when you were talking to my father. I heard everything you said. I love you too, Jake Sullivan."

Jake's breath caught, and instinctively he stepped forward and Lee-two came willingly into his arms. Jake had never kissed a girl before, and the thought had been troubling him some, but he soon found out that it didn't matter.

Epilogue

When seen in the unforgiving light of day, everything about the place had a tired shabby sameness. Ribby cattle with meatless hips and sagging udders, along with their listless calves, scoured the barren hillsides, and were the perfect counterpoint to a careless clutter of weathered, sagging buildings – the sum of which offered little hope for tomorrow. Bathed as it was now in the softer light of the moon, however, the mix of deep shadows and silver light hid the stark ugliness, and the yard looked almost inviting. A short distance to the southeast where the sagebrush and thistles played out at the foot of a steep, gravelly slope, a lone coyote tested the air, then slunk down to disappear into a ragged, dry stream bed. A moment later he reappeared on the opposite bank, and with his nose to the ground, trotted off down the slope on his never-ending quest for food. Then all was still.

Far to the west in the breaks along the Smith River, three men sat cross-legged on the ground, the light of their small fire playing on their faces. The youngest of the three shifted his position slightly to avoid the smoke, and then said, "So you're headed back to Utica."

The man to whom he spoke nodded. He was the oldest of the three, and his heavy moustache was the most notable feature on a weathered face that he'd earned spending long seasons in the outdoors. He squinted slightly as the smoke drifted briefly his way, and the firelight showed up the smile wrinkles that lined his eyes. "There's some interesting country south and west of there," he said after a time. "I'd like to have another look at it."

"Gold?"

"Maybe, but I don't think so. I think there might be something there though."

For a while the men were content with silence, and then the first man spoke again.

"Remember that tight wad saloon owner who threw my paintin' in the wood stove when I tried to buy drinks with it?"

The third man looked up from the fire. "Oliver Carmody," he said with a sour voice. "I don't think he'd be so high and mighty with you now, Charlie."

"Maybe not."

"He sure made me mad though," the third man continued. "I went back in there a couple of nights later an' gave him a bum steer about where he might find some gold. He sure enough had a money hungry look in his eye as I recall."

"Why did you do that, Anson?" The older man asked.

Anson Cramer shrugged his shoulders. "I don't know. I guess I thought maybe it would be fun watchin' the greedy beggar beat himself up tryin' to find it."

"Did he take the bait?"

"I don't know. I ain't been back there for a while. Probably not though. I doubt anythin' came of it."

Made in the USA
Monee, IL
04 April 2021